CRIMSON ALLURE TRILOGY

BOOK ONE
FORBIDDEN

JEZZA DEEP

Copyright © 2025 Jezza Deep
All rights reserved.

DEDICATION

To my brother Jo Jo whose a wild one and does some Forbidden things...

CONTENTS

Chapter 1 6
Chapter 2 10
Chapter 3 20
Chapter 4 32
Chapter 5 41
Chapter 6 46
Chapter 7 57
Chapter 8 69
Chapter 9 80
Chapter 10 90
Chapter 11 97
Chapter 12 101
Chapter 13 107
Chapter 14 117
Chapter 15 124
Chapter 16 132
Chapter 17 142
Chapter 18 149
Chapter 19 158
Chapter 20 161
Chapter 21 169
Chapter 22 178

Chapter 23	188
Chapter 24	198
Chapter 25	204
Chapter 26	212
Chapter 27	217
Chapter 28	226
Chapter 29	234
Chapter 30	238
Chapter 31	246
Chapter 32	254
Chapter 33	261
Chapter 34	268
Chapter 35	276
Chapter 36	285
Bonus Material	290
About the author	291

CHAPTER 1

Life was a playground, and Ryan Dixon had just been kicked off the swing set. Hard. And as if to really drive the point home, life had gone ahead and given him a swift kick to the balls, too. He was still reeling from that one.

A humorless smile tugged at his lips. Normally, he wasn't the kind to wallow. Ryan liked to think of himself as the fun one, the guy everyone wanted to be around. The kind of person who could turn a bad situation into a joke. But here, in this place, even he was losing the will to laugh.

The Pennhurst was a nightmare... no, worse than a nightmare. It was a conspiracy. A trap. A place designed not to fix you, but to finish you off. How was anyone supposed to get better while choking down mashed potatoes that tasted like glue? And the staff? They had to be just as crazy as the patients. After all, who would willingly spend their days here? Ryan could barely last an hour without wanting to claw his way out.

From his spot by the window, he watched a shriveled old man arguing with a baby doll cradled in his arms. The man's voice rose, accusing the doll of sleeping with his wife and stealing all his money. He cocked his head, mildly entertained as the argument escalated into a tirade about all the things his wife apparently wouldn't do for him but happily did for the doll.

"Shoot me now," He muttered under his breath. "If I ever end up like that, just put me out of my misery."

It hadn't been the first time life had thrown him into chaos, but this? This was new. He'd gotten sloppy, ignoring the moon's pull, and keeping the beast locked up for too long. That mistake had landed him here, sedated and strapped down until the full moon passed. Thankfully, no one had noticed the extra body hair, the subtle shifts in his face, his thicker jawline, and the heavy brow. Still, the risk had been too close, and he knew there would be consequences when he got home.

If he got home.

The other patients were proof of how fast things could go downhill in this place. He'd already seen a naked old woman dancing and proclaiming herself a mermaid, a man screaming at invisible attackers, and another guy methodically eating erasers off pencils. Each spectacle only made the walls close in tighter around him.

He needed out. Now.

Spying Nurse Annie Wilkes from Misery—her actual name wasn't worth remembering—he pushed off the wall and jogged over. The woman, all sharp angles and disapproval glared at him with a look so frosty he almost felt his balls shrivel.

"I need to make a call," he said, flashing a smile.

Her thin eyebrows arched. "You told Dr. Barnett you didn't have any family."

"Yeah, well, I was doped up on whatever shit you people gave me. I want my phone call."

Her eyes narrowed, but he held his ground. He saw the flicker of hesitation, the faint trace of fear in her scent. That small victory almost made him grin.

"Fine," she snapped, pointing toward the hallway. "Tell Nurse Sheppard I permitted you. But this is your only call for the week."

His smirk widened as he turned and walked away. "Blow me," he muttered, loud enough for her to hear.

The hallway stretched before him, painted the ugliest shade of baby blue he'd ever seen. It was quiet except for the occasional creak of a wheelchair or the shuffle of a nurse passing by. The phone was just ahead, guarded by a woman who looked like she hadn't moved from her chair in a decade.

Nurse Sheppard, he presumed.

"Hey," he said, tapping on her desk.

She looked up, startled, her pale face flushing as she took him in. He leaned casually against her desk, but when it groaned under his weight he straightened and gestured to the phone.

"Nurse Wilkes said I could make a call."

Sheppard's face turned beet red, and she gestured toward the phone, nearly tipping over in her chair as she shifted her weight. He bit back a laugh, throwing her a wink before walking to the phone.

He dialed quickly, his heartbeat thundering in his ears. The line rang three times before a familiar voice answered.

"Hello?"

Ryan exhaled in relief. "I hope you're sitting down, man, because I'm royally fucked."

"Ryan," came Killian's crisp Irish accent. "What have you done now?"

"Get this... I'm locked up in a loony bin in Pennsylvania, I need you to get me out and fast."

Killian didn't even hesitate. "Give me the address. Harley will be there by morning."

Ryan rattled off the details, his shoulders relaxing for the first time in days.

"Hold tight," Killian added, his tone softening slightly. "We'll handle it."

An hour later, Ryan found himself in the bathroom, nerves buzzing under his skin. He stepped into the last stall, his gaze falling to the collage of magazine clippings, drawings, and scrawled messages covering the door.

And then he saw it.

Taped near the center, in bold, jagged letters ... a single word.... **RUN** "Fuck."

CHAPTER 2

Abbie tried to look at her stay at Pennhurst Asylum with a philosophical lens. It wasn't easy.

She could hate her mother for having her committed. The betrayal had burned, but she grudgingly admitted the truth: without the hospital, she'd likely be dead. Her second suicide attempt would have succeeded. Her wrists bore the scars of her failure—thin, vertical lines that whispered of desperation.

Here, she had her room with a desk and enough art supplies to drown in plus a window that let her glimpse the sun and snow beyond the bars. That view was her lifeline. She told herself that not everyone had even this much. At least here, she was alive.

But the lies still gnawed at her.

Her mother had claimed it was the suicide attempt, her emotional withdrawal, and the grief over her father's death that forced the decision. But she knew better. She'd found the pamphlets for Pennhurst tucked in her mother's dresser weeks before she slit her wrists. Her mother hadn't committed her out of worry or love. She'd done it because Abbie had seen something no one else could explain.

A werewolf.

The memory of that night burned as vividly as fire. A hulking figure covered in black fur with a silver streak, eyes filled with a rage so feral it made her want to crawl out of her skin. It wasn't a wolf, not entirely, but a grotesque fusion of man and beast. Muscled, upright, intelligent, and terrifying, it moved with an unnatural speed and savagery that still haunted her nightmares.

She'd seen it. It had killed her father.

Her doctors called it a delusion, a stress-induced hallucination to cope with the accident, but they hadn't been there. They hadn't seen the beast tearing flesh from a woman's lifeless body like it was nothing more than a family dinner. The way it threw its head back and swallowed a chunk of her, bloody and raw. The sound of bones cracking between its teeth was still lodged in her brain.

The therapists wanted her to let go of the image, to see it as the dream they claimed it was. But how could she forget the creature that had obliterated her life?

Her charcoal scratched across the paper. urgent and precise. She worked on instinct, smudging lines, building shadows, and giving life to her memories. The pill-induced fog tugged at her consciousness, but she ignored it, focusing on her drawing instead.

The werewolf came to life under her hand, every jagged line a testament to her hatred.

It wasn't just the creature itself she loathed. It was everything it represented. It was the reason her father was dead. The reason her body had been broken for months. The reason she was locked up here.

Her gaze drifted toward the window, now framed by a deep indigo sky. Another day slipping into night. Another day lost in the cycle of sleep, drugs, and the suffocating walls of Pennhurst.

...

Across the hospital, Ryan stretched out on the battered common room sofa, arms crossed over his chest as he stared at the muted TV. The night was crawling by, and his nerves itched with impatience. He couldn't wait to get out of this hellhole.

"Hey."

He turned his head toward the voice. Ross, a schizophrenic with a penchant for sharing disturbing gossip, gestured toward the hallway.

"That's your girl."

He frowned and followed Ross's gaze. A pale, frail figure shuffled by the door. Her hair hung in limp tangles, and her hollow eyes were fixed on the floor. She looked like death warmed over.

"That's who drew the picture?" He asked, his hand slipping into his pocket to touch the sketch he'd stolen from the bathroom stall.

Ross nodded eagerly; his face alight with gossip. "Yup. She's the craziest bitch in this place, says a monster killed her dad in some car crash. No one believes her, of course. That's why she's been here for years."

Ryan watched as the girl disappeared down the hallway. "Well, fuck," he muttered.

The visitor's area was an eyesore—a garish explosion of yellow walls and wicker furniture that made Ryan's skin crawl. When Harley stepped through the doors, the ridiculous decor faded into irrelevance.

Ryan rose, grinning. "About damn time."

Harley said nothing, his pale, cold eyes scanning the room before zeroing in on Ryan. The unspoken command in his gaze made Ryan straighten, his grin faltering under the sheer weight of Harley's presence.

Harley wasn't just another Were. He was a killer, pure and simple, wrapped in a deceptively calm exterior. His broad chest and thick arms could uproot trees, but his eyes—glacial, ruthless truly terrified.

Without a word, Ryan led Harley out of the visitor's area and down a quieter hallway. The moment they were alone, he handed over the drawing.

Harley's eyes flicked over the image; his expression unreadable. "Who drew this?"

"A girl," Ryan replied. "Abbie Marsh has been locked up for years and claims she saw a Were."

Harley's fingers tightened around the paper. His voice dropped, low and commanding. "I want to meet her."

Ryan sighed. "Yeah, I thought you would."

Ryan had expected it to be more difficult, but the hospital's vulnerabilities were almost laughable. The electrical system was outdated and crammed into a dusty corner of the basement supply room. Surrounded by boxes of latex gloves and surgical masks, it sat exposed, practically begging to be tampered with.

Ryan obliged. He smashed the metal casing with a wrench, ripped out the ancient wiring, and for good measure, broke the fuses in half. The building plunged into darkness, and the chaos that erupted above was music to his ears.

As he stepped back, wrench slung over one shoulder, he opened the basement door for Harley with a theatrical bow. "Your chariot awaits, my good sir."

Harley didn't dignify the quip with a response, but the faint twitch of his lips was all the approval Ryan needed.

From the moment they reached the women's ward, Harley moved with predator-like precision. The hallways were in disarray—orderlies shouting, patients wailing, the occasional shadow darting across their path but nothing slowed him down.

When they entered Abbie's room, Ryan hesitated at the door.

She lay on the bed, pale and motionless beneath a thin hospital blanket. Her hair was a tangled mess across the pillow, and her fragile frame looked even smaller in the sterile light. The walls around her were papered with her drawings dark, moody pieces that seemed to pulse with life.

Harley strode to her side without pause. His nostrils flared as he inhaled deeply, and for a moment, his expression flickered—something raw and primal beneath his usual calm. Then his jaw set, his pale blue eyes glowing faintly in the darkness.

Harley inhaled deeply again; his body so tense Ryan was amazed it didn't fracture into a million pieces. "What?"

Harley rolled his eyes up, a snarl on his lips. As Ryan watched, his eyes shifted from human to Were. "I want her."

"I hope you're kidding because that's really not funny. We're in a hospital. You can't just fuck a woman while she's out of it." Ryan looked from Harley to the girl, and back again.

"She's my mate! "

His voice was going guttural, but Ryan still understood. And it nearly knocked him over. He raked a hand through his hair, agitation running thick through his veins. Mate? This tiny human was supposed to be his mate? The idea was as preposterous and crazy as the girl supposedly was. And mates were damn hard to find, but who in hell ever thought Harley's would be human? And insane?

"She tried to kill herself. She slit her wrists, Harley. She's not exactly stable." He pinched the bridge of his nose, trying to come up with something. "Are you sure? Her system's so screwed up with the drugs, it's nearly impossible to get a good scent from her. Are you absolutely sure?"

Going completely still, Harley cocked his head and asked darkly, "Are you questioning me?"

Ryan's blood jumped in warning. Solemnly, he said, "No Alpha. I do not question you."

His pale blue eyes, still canine in shape, followed every one of Ryan's movements, and it made him even more nervous. For some reason, Harley had always been far more feral than most Weres. And that meant he was that much more dangerous.

"We're taking her with us."

"Fuck," he muttered under his breath.

They didn't leave through the basement. With Abbie in Harley's arms, they didn't have the luxury of slipping through small windows. Ryan smashed the bars off her room's window instead, the sound muffled by the chaos still raging in the halls.

He kicked the desk aside, shoved the garbage bag filled with her drawings and supplies through the opening, and leaned out to check the drop. No lights. No floodlights outside either, thanks to his handiwork.

"Hand her to me," Ryan said, climbing through the window and landing silently on the grass below. He reached up as Harley passed her unconscious form down, then cradled her awkwardly until Harley landed beside him.

They moved quickly, sticking to the shadows. The car was parked nearby, just a short sprint from the building.

Ryan had barely reached the driver's seat when the emergency exit burst open, spilling three guards onto the lawn. Heavy flashlight beams swept the parking lot, and one landed squarely on the car.

"Shit," Ryan hissed, yanking the door shut and twisting the key in the ignition. The engine roared to life, and one of the guards shouted, pointing toward them.

"Go!" Harley barked.

Ryan threw the vehicle into reverse, the tires squealing as they kicked up gravel. The guards sprinted toward them, their beams bouncing wildly in the dark. Ryan jerked the wheel hard, pulling the car into a sharp turn as they careened across the grass, through a ditch, and onto the road.

The hospital vanished in the rearview mirror, swallowed by the night.

"Jesus," Ryan muttered, his heart still pounding. "Well, that was fun. How the hell are we going to get her home? She doesn't have papers, Harley. This is going to be a nightmare."

His gaze didn't leave Abbie. He held a lock of her hair between his fingers, his expression unreadable.

"Killian arranged it," he said simply. "Drive to the airport."

Ryan glanced at him but didn't argue. When Killian planned, they were as good as law.

The private hangar was small, tucked away from the main terminal. A wiry man met them there, his scent unmistakably Were. He didn't ask questions, barely sparing Abbie a glance as he gestured toward the waiting plane.

Ryan followed Harley onto the aircraft, muttering to himself about the absurdity of the situation. The cabin was cramped but comfortable, and it wasn't long before they were airborne, leaving Pennhurst far behind.

Killian met them at the airstrip near their home. The Lead Alpha stood tall against the biting wind, his silver hair catching the moonlight. Despite his age, his presence radiated authority and power, a stark contrast to the warmth in his eyes as he spotted Ryan.

Ryan dropped the bags and practically tackled him in a hug.

"It's about time you came back to me, boyo," Killian said, his voice rich with affection.

"It's good to be back," Ryan replied, his grin wide despite the exhaustion tugging at him.

They had to wait a few minutes before Harley came out of the building, a bundle of blankets in his arms. He didn't seem to notice the cold or snow as he stepped outside, but he tucked the blankets tighter around the woman bundled within them.

"Tell me everything," he said.

Ryan exhaled and ran a hand through his hair. "I don't know much. She's in her early twenties, was at the hospital for four years, and she's seen a Were. Oh," he added, "and she's human to boot. Can you believe it?"

"My wife was human," Killian murmured, absently rubbing the ring he still wore in her honor. He hadn't removed it since the day she slid it onto his finger.

"I know. But you're you, and Harley is Harley. He's not exactly easy, especially when he's angry or feels threatened. How's a human supposed to deal?"

Killian's voice was sure and smooth as silk. "She'll manage, my boy."

CHAPTER 3

Life floated along smoothly until the drugs began to wear off. Abbie blinked slowly, her mind swimming in a fog. She flexed her fingers against the softness beneath her and frowned. Blankets. Pillows. Fluffy and warm, nothing like the scratchy, institutional bedding she was used to.

Was she dreaming?

She sat up, her muscles sluggish and weak, and looked around. Her hospital room was gone. Instead, she found herself in a cozy bedroom. She'd been lying on a canopy bed, sturdy and elegant, surrounded by dark wood furniture and shelves packed with books. A thick blue comforter pooled around her waist, and a tan-colored carpet muted the sound of her movements as she swung her legs over the side.

She stared at the window. Snow and trees stretched beyond the frosted glass. The world outside was blanketed in white, silent, and still. Wherever she was, it wasn't Pennhurst. It wasn't Pennsylvania.

Her legs shook as she stood but she forced herself upright and shuffled toward the window. Placing her palm against the glass, she recoiled at the sharp chill. It was colder than anything she'd ever experienced. A shiver climbed her spine, not just from the cold, but from the disorienting realization that she had no idea where she was.

Behind her, a voice broke the silence.

"Ah," the man said, his tone warm and easy. "You're awake. And not a moment too soon, either."

She turned slowly, steadying herself against the windowsill. In the doorway stood an older man, his thick silver hair and beard lending him an air of wisdom. Dressed in charcoal pants and a matching sweater, he looked more like a nobleman than anything else. His kind smile didn't quite match the bizarre circumstances.

"Where am I?" Her voice was hoarse, barely above a whisper. "Did someone kidnap me?"

The man hesitated, his smile faltering. "Not...in the traditional sense, no. You're in the Ireland. My sons thought you weren't receiving proper care at the hospital, so we brought you here."

Proper care? Her head spun as she tried to process his words. Who plucked someone out of a mental institution for their own good? Unless…

"Are they doctors?"

"No," he said gently. "But they were concerned."

Concerned? Her suspicion flared, but the effect of the drugs still had her mind clouded. Her legs trembled, and she leaned heavily against the wall.

"Can I go home now?"

"Do you wish to go home?" He tilted his head, studying her closely. "Back to the hospital?"

The words stung, but they held an uncomfortable truth. Did she really want to go back? Her mother's overbearing presence, the monotony of drug-induced stupor, the sterile walls? Still, this wasn't normal. Nothing about it was normal.

"Like you'd let me," she muttered bitterly. "If this is some ransom scheme, you picked the wrong girl. My mother doesn't have any money."

The man sighed. "What would it take to make you feel safe here? Would you like to call your mother? The police?"

Her brows lifted. "The cops? You'd let me call the cops?"

He smiled faintly. "Of course."

Before she could answer, he stepped out and returned moments later with a cordless phone, placing it carefully on the bed. "You'll find it has a dial tone. Call information if you need the number."

She blinked, momentarily stunned. She snatched up the phone and dialed zero, relief washing over her when the operator answered. "Can you connect me to the nearest police station?"

Moments later, a tired voice came through. " Midland Police Station."

"This is the police?" She whispered, gripping the phone tightly.

"Yeah," the man on the other end said. "What can I do for you?"

"I think I've been kidnapped. I—I woke up, and I don't know where I am."

There was a pause, then a sigh. "This a joke?"

"No!" Her voice cracked. "Please, can you trace this number? I don't even know where I am—"

Another sigh, followed by the sound of typing. "Hold on... Oh. You're calling from Killian's place." The tone of suspicion disappeared, replaced with what sounded like mild amusement. "Sweetheart, you haven't been kidnapped. Killian's a good guy. If you want to leave, ask him. He'll probably hand you the car keys and drive you himself also can you please tell him a storm coming?"

The line went dead.

Abbie lowered the phone, her hands trembling. The man from the doorway... Killian stood watching her, arms crossed over his chest.

"You're Killian," she said, her voice small.

He nodded. "Yes."

"The police said to tell you there's a storm coming."

His smile returned, easy and warm. "Thank you, dear. Now, are you satisfied you're safe here?"

It sounded ridiculous when he said it, and even she had to admit it was hard to picture a kidnapper plucking someone out of a psych ward. Her shoulders sagged. "What happens now?"

His expression softened. "Why don't you stay with us for a while? If you're unhappy, we'll arrange something else. But I'd wager you'll find this place a better fit than you expect."

Later, after a much-needed shower and a change into her own clothes, she was still reeling from the discovery that they'd brought her belongings she found herself wandering toward the smell of food.

In the kitchen, Killian moved with the confidence of a seasoned chef, slicing a roast on the counter. Ryan leaned lazily against the wall, a charming smile lighting his face as he saw her.

"Ah, the mystery girl emerges," Ryan said.

Killian glanced up, a smile crinkling his eyes. "Come in, dear. You're just in time for lunch."

Abbie stepped into the room, her nerves prickling at Ryan's attention. He was devastatingly handsome, with tousled brown hair and a cocky air that seemed to fill the room. She hesitated, feeling out of place among their easy familiarity.

Killian, ever the gracious host, gestured toward the dining table. "Why don't you fill the glasses with water? I'll have everything ready in a moment."

Grateful for something to do, she nodded. "Sure."

The meal passed in a haze of conversation and laughter, but tension clawed at her again when a new presence entered the room. The man, Harley moved with a quiet intensity that sent shivers down her spine. His pale blue eyes locked onto hers, unreadable but piercing, and for a moment, she felt like prey caught in a predator's gaze.

Killian introduced him warmly, but she could barely nod in response. Her stomach churned, and when the tension became unbearable, she bolted from the room, her legs carrying her blindly toward the bathroom.

As the door slammed behind her, she could still hear Ryan's voice drawling behind her: "Well, that went well. You're improving, Harley. She didn't pass out this time."

"Ryan," Killian said sharply.

He ducked his head, trying and failing to look apologetic. "Sorry."

Killian sighed, setting his fork down with a quiet clink. "She becomes nervous easily. Harley, I hope you're prepared to be patient. Pushing her will only do more harm than good."

"I'll wait," Harley replied softly, his voice low but resolute.

Killian studied him for a long moment, his sharp eyes catching the steel in his son's pale gaze. He winced inwardly at the determination there. Harley's patience wasn't the question Killian had no doubt his son would wait as long as it took. The real question was Abbie. Would she come to trust them, or would she spiral further into the mistrust and fear born from her past?

Experience had taught Killian one thing: mates didn't always work out.

...

Abbie woke up the next morning more prepared than the day before. The shock of waking up in an unfamiliar place had dulled, though her head still felt foggy. She had her own clothes and her own space, and so far no one had made any threats or condescending remarks. It was...fine.

Except her stomach ached fiercely, a bitter reminder of the previous night's violent retching. When she glanced in the mirror, she groaned. Her face was speckled with blood spots like she'd sprouted dark freckles overnight. Concentrated around her eyes, they gave her the unsettling look of a reverse raccoon.

"Bloody hell," she muttered.

Disgusted, she scrubbed herself clean in the shower. For once, nurses or orderlies did not watch her ready to confiscate her razor at the first sign of hesitation. The privacy was a relief, and even though she still felt raw, the warm water worked wonders on her stiff muscles. She washed her hair twice and borrowed a razor already in the shower to shave.

Wrapped in a towel, she rifled through the dresser, heart-lifting when she found her own clothes neatly folded. She pulled on a long-sleeved undershirt and her favorite jeans, pinning her damp hair into a loose coil. For a moment, she studied her reflection, trying to see herself as someone who belonged in a place like this. She looked like a teenager playing dress-up, still too thin, her face pale beneath the angry red spots.

Not much to work with.

Her stomach growled, breaking the spell. Tiptoeing through the quiet house, she made her way to the kitchen, following the rich scent of coffee. She peeked inside and exhaled in relief when she saw Killian seated at the counter with a steaming cup in hand.

"You're up," she said, stepping cautiously into the room.

He smiled warmly. "Of course, dear. I'm an early riser. Ryan, you won't see before eleven, but Harley is usually about this time. If none of us are around, make yourself at home. Since you skipped dinner yesterday, you must be starving."

"Thanks." She slid onto a stool; grateful he didn't mention her hasty exit last night.

His smile faded as he leaned closer, his brow furrowing. "Are those…spots?"

She flushed and ducked her head, so much for avoiding the subject.

"Uh, yeah," she mumbled. "I kind of get them whenever I…well, when I become ill."

"Hives," He murmured, taking a sip of coffee.

"Yup." She forced a smile, lacing her fingers nervously. "They drove my mom nuts."

"Oh?" His curiosity was evident.

"She wanted me to do pageants," She explained reluctantly. "But I always got nervous before, during, and after. I'd throw up, and then I'd get spots and ruin everything for her. It was awful."

"You didn't enjoy them, then?"

"I hated them." she shook her head vehemently. "But my mom wanted me to do them. She was...invested."

He watched her closely, his gaze soft but thoughtful. Finally, he set his cup down and asked, "What would you like for breakfast?"

"Cereal is fine," she said with a shrug, eager to change the subject.

"You're easy, then," he replied, pulling down a box, bowl, and spoon. "The boys demand a full meal eggs, bacon, potatoes. You name it."

She smiled faintly, taking the items with a murmured thanks.

As she ate, she felt his eyes on her, studying her. It took everything she had not to fidget. Finally, she looked up and blurted, "What?"

He tilted his head, smiling faintly. "Why don't you ask what's on your mind?"

"What makes you think I have questions?"

He chuckled softly. "Because your face is very expressive, my dear. Go on, ask away."

She hesitated spoon poised midair, before lowering it and meeting his gaze. "Where's your wife?"

His smile dimmed. His fingers turned the coffee cup gently as he stared at it. The light caught the gold of his wedding band, still shining despite its age.

"She died," he said quietly. "Many years ago, even before I had Harley."

"You adopted him too?"

"Yes. I found him when he was thirteen, living on the streets of Piraeus. He's been with me ever since."

"So, I'm number three?" she asked, focusing on her bowl.

He raised an eyebrow. "Three what?"

"Rescues," she clarified. "You said Ryan was adopted too, so…"

"You're correct." A small smile returned to his lips. "That makes you number three, although you're a bit beyond the age for legal adoption."

"So, what are you doing with me?" she asked, cutting to the heart of her unease. "You don't even have my records. How are you going to help me without them?"

He sighed, setting his coffee aside. "Child, those medications were killing you. Harley could see it. Ryan could see it. And when they brought you here, so did I. Your illness isn't in your mind it's in the drugs, the environment, and the life they forced you into."

"How do you know that?" she demanded, confused. "You don't know me."

"You're a good girl," he said simply, his tone brooking no argument. "And you'll do fine here. My only concern is whether your body will give out before I can help you heal. Now, finish your cereal."

She frowned but reluctantly took another bite.

He refilled his coffee and glanced at her wrists. "May I ask a question?"

"Sure," she said warily, still chewing.

"Let me see your wrists."

She nearly choked, her spoon clattering against the bowl. "That's not exactly a question."

He gave her a look that was both regal and commanding. "Call it a request, then. Let me see."

Reluctantly, she pulled up her sleeves and laid her hands on the counter, palms up. He slipped on a pair of glasses and leaned in, studying the faint scars that ran vertically along her wrists.

"You did it very precisely," he murmured.

She yanked her hands back and shoved her sleeves down. "Can we talk about something else, please?"

His eyes didn't waver. "Are you going to try it again, Abbie?"

She stilled, caught off guard. Slowly, she shook her head. "Not that I know of."

"Good," he said softly. "I'd hate to be deprived of your company."

CHAPTER 4

Silence lingered in the kitchen as Abbie stared down at her cereal, idly mashing the soggy grains against the side of the bowl. She still felt Killian's gaze, but he didn't press.

"I'll leave you to finish your breakfast," he said gently, breaking the quiet. "Get dressed when you're ready, and afterward, I'll show you around the property. You can ask any questions you have along the way."

She nodded, and he stood, whistling a light tune as he left the kitchen with a spring in his step.

...

Outside, the crisp air-filled Abbie's lungs as she stood on the back porch, staring out over the vast expanse of land before her. Snow-covered hills rolled into the distance, dotted with groves of trees. The world here was still and untouched, a stark contrast to the confining sterility of the hospital.

"So, what is it you guys do here?" She asked as Killian stepped up beside her. "Or does everyone own hundreds of acres just for fun?"

He chuckled. "We like the peace," he said, gesturing for her to follow as he stepped off the porch. "I'm a sculptor if you're asking about my career and I dabble in painting when the mood strikes."

Her eyebrows shot up. "Really? I've never met an artist before."

"Well, now you have."

He led the way as they walked across the snowy property. So far, they had explored the house—three floors of elegant yet functional design, though they'd skipped any rooms currently in use. Outside, they passed the barns, where seven horses watched them curiously from their stalls and a smaller building he called his "storage shed," crammed with everything from old bicycles to broken bird feeders.

He skipped over the garage and another distant structure she couldn't quite make out. She didn't bother to ask about it... yet.

After a short trek through the woods, they stopped at a frozen pond. Its surface shimmered faintly under the weak sunlight, a thick layer of snow covering the ice. She inhaled deeply, savoring the sharp scent of the air. It reminded her of Christmas mornings, the fleeting sense of wonder she used to feel as a child.

He smiled as he watched her. "Shall we return?" he asked. "I'd hate for you to catch a chill."

After their walk back inside the house felt cozier...warmer. She shrugged off her jacket, and Killian took it with practiced ease hanging it in the hall closet.

"I still can't believe how big this place is," she said as they stomped the snow from their boots.

"It's a vast area," He replied. "Many families around here own large parcels of land and the horses enjoy it."

She tilted her head, skeptical. Most people didn't buy hundreds of acres of land just for their horses. But she kept the thought to herself.

"Can I see your studio?" she asked instead, curiosity lighting her features.

He smiled. "If you like."

He led her to the second floor and opened one of the few doors they hadn't explored earlier. She stepped inside and gasped.

"Holy shit." She clapped her hand over her mouth, her cheeks flushing. But the exclamation slipped out before she could stop it.

The room was a masterpiece in itself. Mosaics covered every wall intricate and breathtaking. Forest scenes dominated the space with trees, undergrowth, streams, and dark animals peering out from the shadows. Each wall depicted a different season, the transitions between them so seamless it was as if the room itself breathed with the rhythm of nature.

The vibrant greens of spring melted into the warmth of summer, and golden sunlight dappled through dense canopies. Summer's richness gave way to fiery oranges and reds of autumn, leaves falling like embers. Finally, winter spread across the last wall, its icy blues, and whites stark and beautiful, with faint impressions of wolves in the snow.

She twirled slowly, her eyes wide with awe. "I can't believe you did this," she whispered, her gaze finally settling on him.

He smiled, his hands sliding into his pockets. "I'm glad you like it."

"'Like it' is an understatement."

From the doorway, a familiar voice chimed in. "It's nice, isn't it?"

She turned to see Ryan leaning lazily against the doorframe. His hair was tousled from sleep, and he wore nothing but a pair of boxers.

She quickly averted her eyes, focusing on the mosaics instead.

Ryan drifted into the room, yawning, and stretching. "I was just as shocked when I first saw this place," he said, his grin boyish and charming. "Though I'll admit, I wasn't allowed in until I'd been here for a month."

Killian raised an eyebrow. "You were unruly," he said dryly. "I couldn't risk you taking a marker to my masterpiece."

Ryan laughed, unbothered by the jab. He ruffled his messy brown hair and leaned casually against the wall, his easy confidence stark contrast to Abbie's lingering unease.

She ignored him, her attention drawn back to the mosaics. The detail was incredible every leaf to shadow was rendered with such care it felt alive. For a moment, she forgot about her questions and uncertainty and let herself simply admire the art.

Killian watched her quietly, the faintest hint of satisfaction in his expression.

Taking another look at the murals on the walls, Abbie's attention shifted to the room itself. It was spacious yet simple, clearly designed for utility. A supply cabinet stood against one wall, flanked by a sturdy workbench. An old leather chair, worn into comfort over the years, sat near a potter's wheel in the far-right corner. Across from it was a massive block of clay, wrapped tightly in plastic.

Two easels were set upside by side near a large window at the back of the room, overlooking the snowy woods. The rest of the space was bare, open, and waiting to be filled with creation.

Abbie's gaze fell on a stack of canvases leaning against the wall near the cabinet. Unable to resist, she walked over and picked up the first one. It was a painting of a woman with luscious black hair and a full, shapely figure. She was nude, reclined across the leather chair, her body framed by soft shadows and angles that exuded sensuality.

"My wife," Killian said softly behind her.

Abbie studied the painting for a moment longer, the love in each brushstroke so palpable it felt as though the woman might breathe. "She's beautiful," She murmured, setting the canvas carefully aside.

The next painting showed the same woman standing by a window, her hair pulled into a loose bun and her body clothed in overalls over a white shirt. Her hand rested gently on her swollen belly; her expression serene.

"We lost the baby in the seventh month," he said quietly, answering the unspoken question in Abbie's mind.

"I'm sorry," she said, feeling the inadequacy of the words in the face of such personal grief.

He offered a faint smile. "As I said, it was a long time ago."

The next canvas stopped her cold. It depicted a young man with dark skin and hair, his posture rigid with anger. He leaned against a wall, his eyes fierce and accusing, his displeasure radiating from every stroke of the brush.

"This is your son?" She asked, her voice hesitant.

He nodded. "Harley, not long after I found him. We were still in Greece then."

The intensity of the image made Abbie uncomfortable, as though the boy's frustration was directed at her. She set the canvas aside quickly and reached for the next one only to feel her cheeks burn when she realized who it depicted.

Ryan, unmistakably, sprawled in the same leather chair. He was nude, though strategically positioned, so that nothing explicit was visible. His easy smirk seemed to leap off the canvas, his confidence practically a character in the painting.

Behind her, Ryan laughed.

Her blush deepened as she let out a nervous laugh and placed the canvas back with trembling hands. "I'm surprised you didn't let everything just hang out," she said, darting a glance at him.

Ryan's laughter doubled, rich and unrestrained, as Killian smirked. "Oh, he wanted to," Killian said dryly. "But I wouldn't have it. Women, I love to paint nude. Their forms are graceful and fascinating. But I have no interest in giving intimate detail to a man's cock on my canvas."

Abbie nearly dropped the next canvas, her jaw falling open as her brain struggled to process what she'd just heard.

Ryan slapped his thigh, howling with laughter. "Best line I've ever heard!"

Abbie's embarrassment only deepened as she set the canvas aside and moved on, desperate to find something less mortifying. Thankfully, the remaining paintings were more subdued, though no less striking. One depicted a thin, lifeless girl lying in the street of some foreign country. Another captured a mother breastfeeding her child in a park, her robes open and her face alight with joy.

"They're absolutely wonderful," she said, turning back to Killian with genuine awe. "Perfect. You're brilliant."

"He should be," Ryan quipped, leaning lazily against the supply cabinet. "He gets paid a mint for them."

"And I'm sure they're worth every penny," She retorted without missing a beat, her eyes narrowing at Ryan's smug grin.

As the words left her mouth, something clicked in her mind. A realization swept over her like a tidal wave. She froze, her hand flying to her mouth as her eyes darted to Killian, then back to the stack of paintings.

"Oh my God," she whispered. "I know who you are. I was supposed to go to one of your exhibitions in New York with my art class!"

Her face flushed with embarrassment as the weight of her oversight settled over her. "I can't believe I didn't recognize you. Everyone knows who Killian MacGowen is. You're famous everywhere!"

"Christ," Ryan said, giving Killian an incredulous look. "It took me four years to figure that out. All that time, I thought all you did was murals."

Killian raised an eyebrow. "Really?"

Abbie turned on Ryan horrified. "How could you not know?"

"Hey, I was only eleven when I came here," Ryan shot back, lifting his hands in mock surrender. "Give me a break."

"Besides," Killian said, his tone mild, "I'm not as well-known as you think. I've been fortunate, yes. Galleries and museums have been kind to me, but fame is fleeting."

She shook her head, still grappling with the revelation. The warmth in Killian's demeanor didn't match the larger-than-life figure she'd built up in her mind. The dissonance was jarring and oddly comforting.

Ryan smirked; his arms crossed over his bare chest. "I think you've just had your first celebrity encounter. How's it feel?"

Abbie shot him a glare, her embarrassment flaring anew. "You're insufferable."

"And you're adorable when you're flustered," Ryan replied, his grin widening.

Killian chuckled softly, cutting the tension with his calm presence. "Come now, both of you. Abbie, there's much more to see here than just my work. Let's move on."

She nodded, grateful for the distraction. But as they left the studio, she couldn't help but glance back at the stack of canvases, her mind swirling with admiration, curiosity, and lingering embarrassment.

CHAPTER 5

Killian let her sift through another, smaller stack of canvases. The first was another painting of his wife, her face streaked with tears. The grief etched into her features was so vivid that Abbie's chest tightened in sympathy, an ache that lingered as she set it aside.

The next canvas was of Harley just his face, painted in unflinching detail. His dark eyes blazed with anger; their intensity so raw that she felt an involuntary shiver. She glanced over her shoulder at Killian, who remained quiet, watching her reaction with an unreadable expression.

The rest of the paintings were a mix of scenes from his travels. Some were serene, a quiet village nestled in a valley, a flock of birds in flight against an amber sky. Others were haunting a crowd of mourners in a rain-drenched street, a child sitting alone in an alley, her ribs visible beneath her tattered shirt. Each one was perfect and stirring in its own way, evoking emotions Abbie didn't have words for.

"I'm sorry," Killian said, pulling her attention back to him. "But I don't have any of the sculptures here. I let the last one go about five months ago. Got tired of dusting it." His tone was apologetic but light as if discussing something trivial.

She gave the room a quick sweep with her eyes, taking in its uncluttered, practical design. It made sense. Killian MacGowen was known for being eccentric, even among artists. She remembered learning about his early sculptures in her art class pieces inspired by his wife each sensuous and intimate a celebration of feminine beauty and sexuality. The art world had marveled at him both for his talent and the sheer depth of his devotion to the woman who had been his muse.

"Now," Killian said, walking toward the cabinet, "feel free to make use of anything in this room." He opened the doors to reveal shelves packed with supplies of paints, charcoals, pencils, inks, brushes, and more. "I've seen your sketches, so I know you're comfortable with charcoals and pencils. I've got plenty of those on the third shelf. But if you feel like experimenting, the inks are excellent or the paints." He smiled faintly. "If we run out of anything, I've got extras in the garage."

She stared at the cabinet, her jaw dropping slightly. It was every artist's dream a treasure trove of tools and materials, more than she'd ever had access to in her life.

"Thank you," she said, her voice soft with awe.

From behind her, Ryan groaned dramatically. "Hey, you never let me use your stuff," he protested, attempting to look pitiful.

Killian shot him a sharp glance over his shoulder. "You have no talent."

Ryan clutched his chest in mock offense. "I'm feeling particularly creative today." Swaggering to the cabinet he plucked a black marker from one of the shelves. Turning to Abbie with a mischievous grin, he held it poised above her cheek.

"Let's connect the dots," he said, leaning closer.

"Don't you dare!" Her voice rose in alarm as she stepped back, glaring at him. "That's not even funny, you creep."

"Children," Killian said wearily, though the corners of his mouth twitched with suppressed amusement.

Ryan sighed theatrically and returned the marker to its place. As he headed for the door, his carefree swagger dimmed slightly. "What time tonight?" he asked over his shoulder, his tone more subdued.

"Nine," Killian replied. His voice had shifted, taking on a deeper, commanding timbre that radiated authority.

Ryan stopped in the hallway, his posture stiffening slightly as he nodded. "I'll be there," he said solemnly, his earlier humor entirely gone.

Abbie frowned, watching the exchange with confusion. The playful, irreverent Ryan she'd been dealing with moments ago was replaced by someone almost...obedient.

"What's going on?" she asked once they were alone.

Killian closed the cabinet with a decisive click, turning the handle until it locked in place. He regarded her calmly, his expression softening. "We're going to dinner at the pub tonight," he said. "There'll be neighbors and friends there. I thought it might be nice for you to meet some of them."

Nice wasn't the word she would use to describe the situation. The whole idea of attending dinner with strangers

Killian's friends and neighbors, no less was enough to give her nightmares. A silent prayer to whatever gods might be listening that her stomach would behave for the next twelve hours.

"Won't they think it's a little strange that you just...adopted a stranger?" she asked hesitantly.

"No," he said, his voice calm and assured.

She glanced down at her hands, rubbing her thumb over one of the scars on her wrist. "Do they know where I'm from? Where you found me?"

He sighed softly, his patience unwavering. "They do but none of them will look down on you because of it."

His confidence should have reassured her, but it didn't. A shiver of unease slithered down her spine, tightening its grip on her chest. What if she didn't stay? What would he tell them then? That the troubled girl he'd taken in had run off, proving she wasn't worth the effort?

Another thought struck her like a punch to the gut. Would they think she was some groupie, latching onto the famous Killian MacGowen in a bid for attention or a free ride?

As they left the studio, her mind churned with possibilities. He flipped off the lights and closed the door behind them, his movements deliberate and final.

"Don't worry about dinner," he said, leading her toward the stairs. "The Well has excellent food. You'll enjoy it."

She doubted that very much, but she didn't argue. Thinking about the evening ahead was enough to twist her stomach into knots. She bit her lip, keeping her worries to herself as they descended to the ground floor.

"Now then," he said, pausing in the hallway. "I believe Ryan will be feeding the horses in a few minutes. Why don't you go out and help him?"

She hesitated the weight of the day pressing on her. But the thought of spending time with the horses something steady and nonjudgmental was a welcome distraction. She nodded, grateful for the reprieve.

"Sure," she said quietly.

He gave her a small, approving smile before walking toward the kitchen. She took a deep breath and turned toward the door leading outside. The cold air would be bracing, but it might be just what she needed to clear her head.

CHAPTER 6

Killian waited until Abbie was out of sight before heading out the back door. His steps were steady as he crossed the snow-covered ground toward the one building he'd deliberately kept her away from.

The forge.

The heavy door groaned as he opened it, releasing a blistering heat into the cold. The air inside was thick and acrid, alive with the crackling roar of flames.

Harley stood at the center of the forge, pulling on the rope that controlled the bellows. The fire flared higher with each movement, sending light and shadow dancing across the walls. Sweat slicked his dark skin, dripping from his temples and the cords of his neck, his muscles flexing with each powerful pull.

He released the handle and withdrew a crude iron bar from the fire, its surface glowing molten orange in the dimness. Setting it on the anvil, he picked up a heavy hammer and began to work. The strikes were precise, each blow echoing through the room like a heartbeat. Sparks flew with every impact, but he didn't flinch, his focus absolute.

Killian lingered in the doorway, watching the rhythmic rise and fall of the hammer. Finally, he spoke, his voice calm but purposeful.

"I've called the pack together tonight."

The hammer froze mid-swing. Harley turned his piercing eyes toward his father.

"Does she know?" he asked, his tone low and even.

Killian nodded. "She's nervous about it. She doesn't like being watched, and she's self-conscious about the scars."

He gave a slight nod of acknowledgment and returned to his work, the hammer striking the glowing metal in time with his thoughts. Each blow was smooth and methodical, yet the tension in his movements hinted at an undercurrent of unease.

Killian stepped further into the room, the heat wrapping around him like a living thing. "I'm also going to announce my retirement tonight," he said evenly.

The hammer paused in midair.

"I'll make it official at the next full moon," he continued. "But I want to start preparing the pack now. I'm too old to answer challenges and to be honest, I don't want to anymore. I want to focus on my art…and grandchildren."

Harley let the hammer fall to his side, the weight of his father's words settling between them. His gaze was steady as he turned to face Killian. "Does Ryan know?"

Killian snorted softly. "Lad, most of the pack already knows you'll take my place. They expect it. You're a strong Alpha, Harley. I've never met a Were who could match you."

Harley turned back, thrusting the iron bar into the coals. The fire hissed and spit as it consumed the metal, casting his face in stark relief.

"Jaxon's going to challenge me for it," he said quietly.

"Yes," Killian admitted, his voice tinged with resignation. "And others, I expect. You'll need to be careful. Jaxon doesn't fight fair."

Harley's hands stilled on the bellows. He turned his head just enough to lock eyes with Killian, his gaze cold and unyielding. "If he makes any move, I'll kill him."

The words were delivered with chilling calm, devoid of emotion, but their finality was unmistakable. Killian, though he didn't argue. He knew his son too well. Harley didn't leave things to chance, especially when lives were at stake.

"Call me when I need to get ready," he said, dismissing his father with the same quiet authority that would soon command the entire pack.

Killian inhaled deeply as the crisp; cool air rushed over him as he opened the door. The contrast to the stifling heat of the forge was invigorating, and he lingered for a moment, savoring the freshness. Sweat trickled down his back, soaking into his shirt, but he ignored it. Instead, he turned slightly, glancing over his shoulder at his son.

"She's stronger than I thought," Killian said, his voice thoughtful. "All she needs is time to learn how to live again. To relax. That'll be your biggest hurdle, Harley. But once she trusts you enough to let her guard down."

Harley didn't look up from the fire. His pale eyes were fixed on the leaping flames as he pulled heavily on the bellows. The fire responded with a deafening roar, casting his shadow larger and darker against the walls.

"I won't allow her to leave," he said, his voice low and unyielding.

Killian exhaled quietly, the weight of the declaration pressing against him. He turned fully toward Harley, his gaze steady.

"Hopefully it won't come to that," he replied carefully. "But you'll need to be patient. Be prepared for her to be nervous. Scared, even. She's young, Harley, and being stuck in a hospital, surrounded by doubt and distrust, at such a tender age…" He trailed off, shrugging lightly, as if to say it was a wound not easily healed.

"I won't let her leave." his voice came again, harder this time, like steel striking stone. He turned to meet Killian's gaze, the firelight dancing in his pale blue eyes. "I won't."

Killian studied him for a long moment, his expression softening with a father's understanding. "I know," he said quietly leaving.

...

By the time they finished in the barn, Abbie hardly noticed the cold. She was flushed and warm from brushing the horses, hauling feed, and struggling with the pitchfork under Ryan's teasing instructions.

"You need muscle," he said with a cheeky grin, effortlessly taking the pitchfork from her hands. Abbie, panting too hard to reply, just glared at him.

Still, when they were done, the barn was spotless, and she knew all seven horses by name. She adored each one, from the spirited gelding that had tried to nibble her jacket to the older mare she couldn't stop petting.

"Who rides them?" she asked, running her hand over the bay mare's sleek neck.

"I used to," Ryan replied, offering a chunk of apple to the gelding, who eagerly snapped it up. "But I haven't in a while. Harley and Killian never really learned. Plus," he smirked, "the horses don't like either of them. They make them nervous."

"Huh." she frowned, imagining Killian making anyone nervous. Harley, sure. But Killian? Impossible.

When they finally trudged back to the house, it was nearly six, and both were covered in snow. Abbie's hair was frozen in clumps thanks to Ryan's enthusiastic push into a snowdrift. Snow had also leaked down her jacket, chilling her back. But somehow, none of it mattered. For the first time in ages, she felt…normal.

It didn't feel strange to treat Ryan like a brother. He naturally fell into that role, teasing her mercilessly that felt safe and affectionate. She appreciated it. She understood him, his charm, and easy confidence, and he indulged in women like they were his favorite pastime. She liked that he didn't look at her that way.

Killian met them at the door, his sharp eyes taking in their disheveled state with a sigh. "To the showers. Both of you. And Ryan," he added, his voice deepening with mock sternness, "you had better be ready in an hour. I refuse to have a son who takes longer to dress than most women."

Ryan grinned and flipped him the bird before bounding up the stairs two at a time. Abbie couldn't help but laugh at his exuberance, despite herself.

Killian shook his head, watching his son disappear. "He's always been a handful, that one."

She shrugged as she slipped off her jacket. "He's funny. A little immature, sure, but funny."

His mouth quirked into a smile. "I'm glad you enjoyed the barn. Now, go get cleaned up, hmm?"

With a nod, she handed over her coat and headed to her room.

Once inside, she closed the door firmly and surveyed her meager wardrobe with a sigh. What was she supposed to wear to meet new people when her choices were limited?

Most of her clothes were thin, long-sleeved undershirts paired with T-shirts featuring rude or sarcastic slogans. As much as she liked the irony, insulting a room full of strangers, Killian's friends didn't seem like the best idea. The last thing she wanted was to make him look bad.

She dug through her small pile of clothes, eventually settling on a purple long-sleeved shirt. It wasn't fancy, but it was the best she had. She'd never worn it before; her mother had given it to her during her first Christmas at the hospital, and it had sat untouched ever since. She paired them with her only decent jeans, hoping they would be good enough for a casual pub.

With a worried glance at her reflection, she grabbed a towel and headed for the shower.

...

The drive to the pub was mercifully short, just ten minutes through winding forest roads. Abbie sat in the back seat, nerves jangling in her chest as the car bumped along the gravel driveway.

The pub came into view, a low, weathered building surrounded by trees. It's rough exterior, darkened by years of harsh weather, made it clear this was no fancy establishment. For a fleeting moment, her anxiety eased.

Ryan jumped out first, bounding around the car to open her door with an exaggerated bow. "Milady," he said, his grin wide and playful.

She slid out, her eyes darting toward the building. The lot was nearly full, with vehicles parked in haphazard rows. She wrapped her arms around herself, shivering.

"Looks like most everyone's here," he said, scanning the cars.

Her stomach sank at the implication. A lot of people. Too many.

Killian emerged from the passenger side, his steady presence grounding her nerves. She instinctively gravitated toward him, needing the comfort of his calm authority before facing the crowd inside.

The drive itself had been nerve-wracking enough. Harley had driven, his expression as dark and unreadable as ever. He hadn't said a word the entire way, but his disapproving silence had been oppressive.

Now, standing in the crisp evening air, she swallowed her nerves and fell into step behind Killian as he led the way to the pub.

Killian held the door open for her, leaning down to murmur, "Don't be nervous. They're all very friendly."

She nodded, forcing her legs to carry her inside, though every instinct screamed at her to turn and run.

She took a deep breath and stepped inside.

The warmth hit her first, carrying the rich smell of hot food, beer, and the faint tang of woodsmoke. The pub had a distinct charm, its wooden interior darkened with age and polished smooth from years of use. Soft music played in the background, blending seamlessly with the low hum of conversation.

It wasn't the rowdy, antler-decked kind of place she half-expected, but it still had a rustic, lived-in feel. She relaxed slightly, only to freeze again when she realized everyone was staring at them.

Dozens of eyes turned toward the door. Some were curious, others openly appraising, and all seemed to shift immediately to Killian.

He stepped up beside her, scanning the room with a practiced ease. He nodded toward a group of men near the bar.

"Shane, Ronan," he called, his voice warm. "How are you?"

Two men broke away from the crowd and approached with broad smiles, their hands outstretched. He greeted them each with a firm handshake and a quick embrace, their easy camaraderie clear.

They must be close, she thought, watching the exchange.

But before she could dwell on it, what seemed like half the pub surged toward them, murmuring greetings and patting Killian on the back. The air filled with a soft buzz of Gaelic, words slipping by too quickly for her to catch. The crowd pressed in, pulling Killian deeper into the room like a tide sweeping him away.

It was overwhelming.

She stepped back instinctively, her heel bumping into something solid. She turned to find herself face-to-face with Harley, his pale eyes watching her intently. Her pulse jumped as she tried to stammer an apology, but he didn't move, his presence unyielding.

"Don't worry," Ryan's voice whispered suddenly in her ear, making her flinch. He was on her right, leaning close enough to speak without being overheard. "Just hang back. No one's going to bother you. When he introduces you, just nod. You'll be fine."

She nodded stiffly, gripping her hands together to stop them from trembling. He was right. She was acting ridiculous. It was just meeting new people, nothing to be scared of.

Taking a steadying breath, she forced herself to relax.

"Come on," Harley said, his voice low and commanding. He motioned for her and Ryan to move.

Ryan glanced to the left and immediately grinned. "Hey, I'm going to go say hi to Lorcan." With a cheerful wave, he disappeared into the crowd, leaving Abbie's heart sinking in his wake.

"Come," Harley repeated. This time, his arm slid firmly around her waist, guiding her forward whether she wanted to go.

Her breath hitched at the sudden contact, a shiver of unease rippling down her spine. But there was no room for argument. He moved with purpose steering her to a table near the center of the room where Killian was already seated.

She sat down where he indicated, her heart hammering. Rather than taking the chair across from her, he sat beside her, his presence impossible to ignore.

Killian smiled at her from across the table, his calm demeanor; a small comfort. Another man took the seat next to him, and a third dragged over a chair to sit at the end of the table.

Abbie recognized the man at the end Shane, one of the first Killian had greeted. He was large and middle-aged, with kind eyes that immediately put her at ease.

"You'll introduce me, Killian?" Shane said with a smile, winking playfully at her.

Before Killian could reply, Harley's smooth voice cut through the moment like a blade.

"She's not his to introduce," he said, his pale eyes locking on Shane.

The shift in tone was immediate. Shane's smile faltered, and he straightened slightly in his chair, his expression wary. The tension that rippled through the table was subtle but undeniable.

"My apologies," he said carefully, inclining his head toward Harley. "Would you please perform the introductions?"

CHAPTER 7

She watched the exchange, her irritation bubbling up alongside her confusion. The tension between Harley and Shane was palpable, and the abrupt shift into Gaelic left her completely in the dark.

Her frustration emboldened her, and before she could overthink it, she stuck out her hand. "Hi. My name's Abbie Marsh. I'm staying at Killian's for the week, maybe a little longer."

Shane's discomfort was obvious, but he took her hand with a polite smile.

"Nice to meet you, Abbie. You can call me Shane." He dropped her hand quickly, his gaze darting toward Harley as though seeking permission for even that brief interaction.

Killian broke the awkward silence, his tone calm but carrying a note of caution as he addressed his son in Gaelic. *"Harley, she doesn't understand."* His sharp eyes moved between Shane and Harley. *"You're already confusing her with your behavior."*

Harley didn't flinch. His eyes remained locked on Shane's, cold and unyielding. *"She's mine, Shane. Be sure to tell the others."*

Shane's shoulders stiffened, and after a tense pause, he dropped his gaze and nodded. *"Yes, Alpha."*

The quiet acknowledgment sent an uneasy ripple through Abbie. Alpha? What the hell was that supposed to mean?

Killian turned to her with a smile, cutting through the tension. "What would you like to drink?" he asked, switching back to English.

She hesitated, glancing around the table. Something about the way the other man, the older one seated next to Killian refused to meet her eyes added to her unease. His thin frame and weathered features reminded her of a sparrow, and yet he exuded a quiet wariness that made her stomach tighten.

"Abbie," Killian prompted gently.

"Water with lemon, please," she said, unable to keep the edge of irritation from her voice. She hated being shut out of the conversation, especially when it felt important.

Killian nodded and rose from the table, walking toward the bar. Abbie tried to make sense of the moment, her mind circling back to the strange exchange between Harley and Shane. What the hell had that been about?

"Ryan seems well," the older man murmured suddenly, breaking the silence. His eyes remained fixed on the table, his voice low and cautious.

Beside her, Harley gave a single nod. "He is."

"Will he be staying this time?"

"Yes. His wandering is over."

"Just in time for Killian's retirement then," Shane said.

Abbie's brows furrowed. Retirement? She filed the comment away for later, unsure if she'd have the nerve to ask what it meant.

Before she could dwell on it, Killian returned, balancing three glasses. Ryan followed closely, carrying three more. They set the drinks on the table, Ryan's grin as wide and carefree as ever as he pulled over a chair and claimed the unoccupied end of the table.

"It's good to see you, Ryan," the older man said, lifting his glass in greeting.

"You too, Ronan." he raised his glass in response, then took a long sip of his nearly black beer.

Abbie frowned at the sight. "What are you drinking?" she asked, unable to hide her distaste.

Ryan held up his glass like it was a trophy. "Guinness, princess. Wanna try it?"

"Um, no thanks." Her nose wrinkled involuntarily. The thick, dark liquid looked more like tar than something meant for drinking.

He chuckled, licking the foam from his upper lip. "You know, you turned twenty-one while you were cooped up. Didn't even get the chance to celebrate being legal. And here, the drinking age is nineteen. Live a little."

"I'm fine," she replied firmly, pulling her water closer. "I'm good with this."

Shane gave her a conspiratorial smile. "You don't want that stuff anyway, Abbie. It'll make you sink to the floor it's so heavy."

"Are you insulting my taste in beer?" Killian asked with mock indignation, raising a brow.

"God, no." Shane chuckled. "If anything, you've got my respect for being able to drink that stuff. I just can't figure out how you do it."

The tension at the table began to ease as the conversation shifted to lighter topics. The men swapped stories about hunting, the recent snowstorms, and the large buck that had been spotted in the woods near the property.

She listened quietly, doing her best to blend in. She stirred the lemon in her water with the straw, letting her eyes wander around the pub.

The people seated at the other tables were a mix of ordinary locals, dressed in faded jeans, sturdy boots, and heavy flannel shirts. The room was filled with laughter and the hum of conversation, most of it in Gaelic. She picked out a few low-spoken phrases in English, but they were too quiet to catch clearly.

Her eyes swept over the room, noting that the crowd was mostly men. The few women scattered among them seemed comfortable but reserved, sticking close to their companions. Was this just how the area was? Sparse on women? Or was there something else that made them avoid places like this?

She took another sip of her water, letting the questions swirl in her mind. Everything about tonight felt like it had layers she didn't fully understand.

"Abbie…"

"Hm?" She blinked, dragging her gaze away from the other patrons. Something about the room, about everyone here, felt…off. It was like there was a layer of meaning beneath every word spoken, every glance exchanged. She couldn't put her finger on it, but the feeling left her unsettled.

Lost in her thoughts, she flinched when a firm hand grasped her chin, gently but insistently turning her head. Suddenly, Harley filled her vision, his pale eyes boring into hers with an intensity that made her stomach flip.

"What will you have for supper, Abbie?" His voice was low, rumbling, as if gravel scrapped against steel. There was a rawness to it like he hadn't spoken enough that day or perhaps ever.

"I'm not hungry," she mumbled, pulling slightly back.

His jaw tightened, and something sharp flashed in his eyes, a cold anger that only made his gaze more chilling. "What will you eat?" he repeated, his tone leaving no room for refusal. "You *will* eat, Abbie."

Her pulse jumped, her thoughts spinning. Why did he care? Why was he so insistent?

Swallowing, she nodded reluctantly. "Soup," she whispered. "Soup will be fine."

His fingers slipped away, leaving a lingering heat on her skin. He turned toward the waiter, Riley, who stood nearby with a notepad.

"Vegetable, beef, or chowder?" Riley asked, his pen poised.

"Vegetable," she said, her voice soft.

He scribbled it down, then looked at her expectantly. "And?"

Ryan propped his chin on his hands, smirking at her like this was the most entertaining thing he'd seen all night.

"Th-that's all," she stammered.

Harley fired off a quick, sharp command in Gaelic. Riley's eyes darted to him, then back to her. With a cautious nod, he jotted something down before moving to Killian, who ordered fish with the ease of a man completely at home.

The conversation shifted back to Gaelic, and she sank into her chair, content to let their words wash over her like background noise. The tension from earlier seemed to ease as the men spoke, their tones ranging from casual to clipped as they debated something she couldn't understand.

Ryan leaned back in his chair, equally detached from the conversation, his smirk still playing at the edges of his mouth. She took some comfort in that, at least she wasn't the only one sitting out.

When the food came, Riley handed out massive plates to everyone. Her bowl of vegetable soup was accompanied by a plate holding a towering ham sandwich, a scoop of potato salad, and a large dill pickle.

"I didn't order this," she said, staring at the plate like it might bite her.

His eyes flicked nervously to Harley before he answered. "He got it for you."

"Eat it," Harley said firmly, taking his plate of steak flanked by roasted potatoes, carrots, and a lobster tail.

"At least try," Killian added mildly as he tucked into his fish.

Ryan, sitting across from her, muffled his laughter behind his arm. She glared at him, sticking her tongue out like a petulant child. That only made him laugh harder.

Sighing, she pushed the sandwich aside and started on the soup. It was surprisingly good, thick, and savory, with chunks of fresh vegetables in a tomato-based broth. The slab of sourdough bread served alongside it was almost comically large, but she nibbled at the edge. She kept stealing resentful glances at the untouched sandwich, feeling ridiculous for holding a grudge against food.

The men's conversation shifted again, drawing her reluctant attention.

"Jaxon's not going to like it," Shane said, tearing into a piece of bread. "Neither will his uncle."

Killian shrugged, his tone calm but resolute. "Then he can challenge just like anyone else who thinks they'll do a better job."

"You'll need to be careful of that one, boy." The older man next to Killian finally spoke, his voice dry and weathered, his sharp gaze fixed on Harley. "Jaxon's as likely to shoot you in the back as he is to challenge you outright. Or worse, he'll let the others go first, hoping to wear you down."

Harley didn't flinch. If anything, he looked bored. "Let him try," he said softly. His words carried a weight that silenced the table for a moment. "I can take it."

The older man studied Harley for a long moment before nodding, as if satisfied.

Abbie stirred her soup absently, pretending not to listen. But her mind whirled with questions. What was this "challenge" they kept mentioning? Why was it such a given that Harley would be the one to face it?

And what kind of world had she walked into, where a man like Harley could say such things with the cold certainty of someone who had already faced it all and won?

She laid her spoon aside, raising a brow at Killian. His only response was a genial smile as he speared another bite of fish and chewed contentedly.

The conversation at the table continued, growing even more cryptic as the men delved into topics like "clan rights" and "structure." They spoke with a familiarity that excluded her completely, their words heavy with meaning she couldn't decipher. Halfway through, they switched to Gaelic.

Her patience snapped. With a sigh, she pushed her soup bowl away and slumped back in her chair.

"You didn't eat your sandwich," Harley said.

His voice cut through the conversation like a knife. The low hum of Gaelic stopped abruptly, every man at the table turning to watch.

Abbie's gaze flicked from her barely touched soup to Harley's empty plate. He'd cleaned it with military precision, even mopping up the juices from his steak with a piece of bread.

"Eat your sandwich, Abbie," he said again, his tone flat yet commanding.

Her eyes dropped to the offending sandwich, sitting innocently on its plate as though it hadn't caused her any grief. *Is it possible to resent a sandwich?* she wondered idly. The feeling was absurd but real... an echo of her childhood, of sitting in her mother's kitchen while enduring the torture of curlers and makeup for pageants she despised.

"No," she said finally, her voice quiet but firm.

He turned slowly, his pale eyes locking on her with unnerving focus. "Did you say something?"

He asked it so calmly as if he were inquiring about the weather. Yet, there was steel beneath the words, a chilling expectation of obedience that sent a flutter of unease through her.

For a moment, the fear rose, a bird fluttering frantically in her chest. But then irritation surged up and drowned it out. She had spent years being pushed around, following orders from people who had no right to dictate her life. Where had obedience gotten her? Locked in a hospital with no freedom, no voice, and no hope.

Staring back at him, her voice wavered slightly, but she stood her ground. "No, thank you. I'm not hungry."

"Abbie..." His tone was low and dangerous, a rumble that prickled at her skin.

The warning should have cowed her, but instead, it sparked something rebellious in her. That voice, so commanding, so assured made her want to fight.

She straightened, the edges of her anger sharpening as she bit out, "*You* ordered it. *You* can eat it."

Her heart thundered in her chest, her pulse racing so fast it made her dizzy. But at the same time, there was a heady rush of triumph. Disobeying felt exhilarating.

Harley's gaze darkened, and the corner of his mouth twitched into a scowl. "Of all places, you challenge me here," he growled, his voice laced with quiet fury.

She flinched just slightly but clung to her courage like a lifeline. "I don't want it," she said, her voice firmer now.

The atmosphere at the table shifted. The other men stopped pretending to eat, their gazes flicking nervously between Abbie and Harley.

"Alpha..." Shane spoke carefully, his voice a soft plea for peace.

Harley's eyes slid toward him, a slow, deliberate movement. Whatever Shane had been about to say died in his throat. He nodded in submission and stared down at his plate.

Alpha.

The word hung in the air, foreign and absurd. Who even *called* someone that? And why did he think it was his right? She wanted to scoff, to dismiss the ridiculous title outright, but the tension in the room was suffocating.

Her hand trembled as she pushed the plate toward him. "Enjoy," she said, her voice a mocking imitation of politeness.

For a moment, she was certain he was going to yank her out of her chair and snap her neck. Her breath hitched, and the fight-or-flight instinct screamed at her to run.

But then he moved not toward her, but toward the sandwich. He picked it up and took a large, deliberate bite, chewing slowly as his eyes remained locked on hers.

The others at the table relaxed visibly, though no one dared comment.

"Well," Killian said, his tone dry as he set down his fork. "Does anyone have any other worries or concerns?"

No one answered. The men shook their heads in silence, avoiding Killian's gaze.

Killian clapped his hands together once, a brisk sound that shattered the lingering tension. "Excellent. In that case, I'll take Abbie with me and introduce her to the others." He stood, smiling at Abbie. "I'll see you all tomorrow."

She pushed back from the table, eager to escape. She followed Killian without a backward glance, her pulse still hammering in her ears.

He leaned down as they stepped from the table to murmur, "You're braver than I thought, child. That was…unexpected."

"Was it?" she asked, her voice tight as she struggled to calm herself.

He chuckled; his tone dry. "Oh, very much so."

Behind her, she could feel Harley's gaze boring into her back, the weight of his attention making her shoulders stiffen. But she didn't turn around. Whatever game she had just entered, she wasn't about to back down now.

CHAPTER 8

She drifted into consciousness, warmth pressing against her from all sides. She blinked groggily and realized strong arms held her close against a broad, muscled chest.

Her first reaction was confusion, and her body stiffened against the unexpected intimacy. Then it all came rushing back: She was in Ireland, at Killian's home. She had fallen asleep on the drive.

When she tried to move, the arms tightened around her like iron.

"Don't," Harley's voice rumbled above her, deep and commanding.

Too tired to argue and too worn out to summon bravery, she gave up and sagged against him. The fight that had felt so exhilarating earlier now seemed foolish in hindsight. She let her head fall back against his chest, the steady thump of his heartbeat oddly soothing.

He carried her silently through the house, the dim light casting his shadow long and foreboding on the walls. When they reached her room, he pushed the door open with his foot and stepped inside, cradling her like she weighed nothing at all. He laid her gently on the bed, his hands moving to remove her boots.

For a moment, he hesitated, leaning over her. In the faint light from the hall, his face was heavily shadowed, his sharp features taking on a demonic edge. She wanted to ask him what he was doing and why he was lingering, but sleep claimed her before the words could form.

The next morning, she woke early, her body refreshed despite the odd dreams that lingered at the edges of her mind. After dressing quickly, she made her way to the kitchen and helped herself to a bowl of cereal. The house creaked in the winter wind, but the sounds didn't unsettle her. For the first time in a long while, she felt a faint sense of ease, as though she were slowly reclaiming a piece of herself.

After breakfast, she made her way to the studio. The sight of the art supplies, perfectly organized and abundant, filled her with a quiet excitement. Pulling out a large sketch pad and a set of charcoals, she settled onto a stool and let her hands take over. The lines came quickly, her strokes bold and heavy, until the shape of her subject began to emerge.

She became so consumed and lost in her work that the hours slipped unnoticed.

Killian woke to the faint scent of charcoal and Abbie's now-unpolluted scent lingering in the air. He smiled softly as he climbed out of bed. The girl was proving to be resilient. Stronger than he had anticipated.

After giving her a few hours, he climbed the stairs and knocked on the studio door.

"Abbie?" he called.

There was no answer. Frowning, he opened the door silently and stepped inside.

She was slumped over the workbench, her head resting on one arm while the other dangled loosely, her fingers stained black with charcoal. Her hair was loose down her back, soft waves catching the muted light streaming through the window. Killian took a moment to study her—her face was no longer gaunt, her eyes less haunted. She looked...alive again.

At the sound of his steps, she stirred, lifting her head groggily. "Hmm?"

Killian's gaze drifted to the sketch she had been working on, and he froze.

"Where did you see this?" His voice was calm, but there was a sharpness to his tone that made her blink.

She stiffened. "I don't know," she said, her tone wary. "Probably dreamt it."

He leaned closer, studying the page. The drawing was unmistakable—a Were in mid-shift, its fur bristling, teeth bared in a snarl. The detail was uncanny, down to the gleam of its claws and the feral intelligence in its eyes.

"Well," he said lightly, masking his unease, "it's well done. Perhaps you should try painting it."

She frowned at the sketch and then shoved it aside with a shrug. "I think I'm done for the day." She began cleaning up her supplies, her movements brisk.

"If you wouldn't mind," he said, "I could use your help in the kitchen."

"Sure."

They worked side by side, falling into an easy rhythm. He regaled her with tales of his travels, his rich voice weaving stories of distant lands—Egypt, Spain, Italy. She listened with rapt attention, occasionally laughing at his more absurd anecdotes.

When they finished preparing lunch, the counter was piled with thick, overstuffed sandwiches, containers of potato salad, and a jar of pickles.

"These are enormous," she said, eyeing the sandwiches with skepticism. "Are you sure they're not too big?"

He chuckled. "They're just fine. Wrap these if you don't mind."

She nodded and began wrapping the sandwiches in plastic.

When everything was packed, he hefted a zippered bag onto the counter. He added the food containers and then, almost as an afterthought, dropped an apple inside. "That should do it."

She tilted her head curiously as he handed her the bag.

"Would you be a dear and take this out to the far building?" he asked, gesturing toward the structure she hadn't seen before.

He dropped the strap of the bag on her shoulder and turned away, already mumbling about supper.

After donning her coat and boots, she entered the cold and promised herself that next time she'd refuse, except she knew she wouldn't. So far Killian hadn't made her angry enough to refuse him anything, and it seemed that she was too much of a pushover to be rude without the anger.

The trek to the building felt endless. The snow was thick, clinging to her jeans and soaking through her boots. By the time she reached the door, her legs were numb, her teeth chattering so hard she was surprised they hadn't cracked. She stared at the small window at the north end of the building, glowing orange like the eye of a beast. Thick smoke churned from the chimney, swirling upward into the stark, gray sky. Whatever Harley was doing in there, she was certain of one thing—it was warm.

Shivering violently, she raised her fist and pounded on the door. The sound of her knocking was muffled by the wind. She waited a beat, stomping her feet to keep the blood circulating. When no answer came, she raised her hand to knock again, but the door was wrenched open before her fist could connect.

The heat hit her like a wall, nearly knocking her back. He stood in the doorway, shirtless, his dark skin gleaming with sweat. The cold wind whipped around him, making the sweat glisten like droplets of molten metal. For a moment, she couldn't tear her eyes away. His chest was massive, broad, and powerfully muscled, the deep ridges of his abdomen sharp enough to cut glass.

Her mouth went dry.

"Lunch," she croaked, her voice embarrassingly thin against the roar of the wind. She tugged at the strap slung over her shoulder, her hands trembling not entirely from the cold.

His pale eyes narrowed, pinning her in place like a predator sizing up its prey. "Come in," he said, his voice a low rumble that sent a shiver down her spine. He stepped aside, holding the door open wide enough for her to enter.

She hesitated, clutching the strap of the bag like a lifeline. The biting wind tore at her back, while the promise of warmth beckoned from inside. Swallowing her nerves, she stepped over the threshold. Heat enveloped her immediately, a smothering embrace that made her cheeks flush. The heavy door shut behind her with a metallic clang, cutting off the outside world.

The building was dim, lit only by the pulsing glow of flames in the fire pit. Shadows danced wildly across the walls, twisting, and writhing in time with the crackling of the fire. Her gaze flitted over the unfamiliar equipment that filled the space with massive hammers, strange tongs, and other tools she couldn't begin to name.

"What is this place?" she asked, her voice barely above a whisper.

"A forge," he replied, his tone clipped. He reached out and slipped the bag from her shoulder, his fingers brushing against her coat. She stiffened but said nothing, watching as he set the bag down on a workbench and unpacked its contents with precise, deliberate movements.

She stayed rooted in place, awkward and unsure. The oppressive heat and his looming presence made her feel small and out of place. She glanced toward the far end of the room, searching for an escape from the tension.

"Is it okay if I…" She gestured vaguely toward the other side of the forge. The words stuck in her throat, and she let her arm drop.

For a fleeting moment, she thought he might smile. The corners of his mouth twitched, and something almost like amusement flickered in his eyes. But just as quickly, it was gone, replaced by his usual stern, unreadable expression.

"Of course," he said, his voice softer this time. He returned to the food, meticulously unwrapping sandwiches and setting them in neat rows on the workbench.

She moved deeper into the forge, her curiosity overtaking her discomfort.

The air was heavy with the scent of smoke and hot metal, tinged with something earthy and metallic. Tools of every shape and size lined the walls, hanging on thick iron hooks. Some looked ancient, their surfaces darkened with age and wear, while others gleamed like they'd been crafted yesterday.

Near the fire pit, a large bellows hung from the ceiling, its rope swaying gently. She traced its length with her eyes, marveling at the simplicity of its design. Bundles of twisted metal were scattered throughout propped against walls, piled in corners, and even balanced precariously across the rafters.

But it was the weapons that stopped her in her tracks.

There were five swords, each exquisitely crafted, their blades long and elegant, nearly as tall as she was. They looked like they belonged in a museum, displayed alongside other relics of a long-forgotten era. Every inch gleamed with care and precision, betraying the meticulous hand of their maker. Alongside the swords hung a collection of axes, their curved edges brutal yet artful, a pike that seemed fit for a king's guard, and a variety of knives ranging from sleek and practical to outright terrifying.

Her fingers hovered near the hilt of a particularly beautiful sword, its guard inlaid with a swirling pattern of silver and gold. She didn't dare touch it, but the urge was there. What kind of person owned weapons like these?

"You challenged me last night."

The deep rumble of his voice startled her. She glanced over her shoulder, catching him mid-bite of his second sandwich. He leaned lazily against the bench, his sweat-slicked chest rising and falling with each breath, all power and sinew wrapped in a thick layer of menace.

It was maddening how attractive he was—big, broad, and carved from muscle. The faint sheen of sweat only added to his appeal, though the danger he radiated ensured she could never forget how much of a predator he truly was.

Turning back to the swords, she schooled her face into neutrality. "I'm sorry." The words came out flat and unconvincing. Her inner voice was quick to chime in with a victorious *No, I'm not!*

The memory of the pub flickered in her mind, and despite the tension that had followed, she'd felt more alive in that moment than she had in years.

"You made all of these?" she asked, gesturing toward the weapons to shift the focus of their conversation.

"Through the years, yes."

She traced the sharp lines of an axe with her gaze, admiring its brutal simplicity. "So, that's what you do here? Make swords and knives and...other things?" The hesitation in her voice betrayed her uncertainty about some of the more obscure tools she'd seen.

Silence stretched between them.

After a moment, she heard the soft creak of leather as he shifted. Heavy footsteps followed, measured and deliberate, and he closed the distance between them.

He stopped directly in front of her, blocking her view of the weapons.

His presence loomed over her, his proximity stealing the air from her lungs. She instinctively stepped back, but his low voice, filled with quiet command, froze her mid-step.

"Don't."

Her body stiffened. The single word had been neither loud nor sharp, yet it struck her with the force of a whip crack.

"And yes," he said, his pale eyes fixed on hers, their intensity unnerving. "That is what I do here."

She swallowed, her throat dry. "What?"

"You will not do that again." His voice was a growl, the meaning behind his words clear.

It clicked—the pub. He was talking about the pub. About her refusal to obey.

Her fingers twitched at her sides, the memory of her small rebellion both thrilling and nerve-wracking. She had never stood up to anyone the way she had stood up to him. She hadn't just faced the fire; she'd walked straight into it.

"I..." she began, then stopped herself. What could she say? That she'd meant it? That she'd do it again?

"Next time you get your back up," he continued, his tone deceptively calm, "you will have to deal with me afterward."

Her stomach twisted at the implied threat or was it a promise? She nodded reflexively, though a rebellious voice screamed at her to defy him again. *Why should he get to decide? What does he have that I don't?*

But deep down, she knew the answer: everything. Strength. Authority. A presence that demanded compliance.

She held her tongue, refusing to give him the satisfaction of an apology.

"You can go."

He turned from her dismissively, his attention returning to the half-finished sandwich on the bench.

Relieved but bristling, she made her way to the door. The heat from the forge clung to her skin, making the frigid air outside feel like a slap to the face when she stepped into it.

As she trudged back through the snow, her mind buzzed with a single thought: she had to sketch him.

CHAPTER 9

She was quiet throughout the lunch meal. Ryan looked at her, detected Harley's scent, and knew where she'd been. After deciding to give Harley a few hours to cool off, he visited the forge later that afternoon.

Unlike Killian, he didn't mind the heat of the place. He breathed in the smell of hot metal and sweat like it was perfume and stripped his shirt. He got an extra leather glove off the bench and waited for orders. Harley didn't waste any time.

"Man, the bellows for me while I work on this."

For the next half hour, neither of them spoke. Ryan pulled on the rope that operated the airflow to the fire while Harley pounded the shit out of the metal, alternating between two different pieces.

"Are you still sure she's your mate?" he asked, taking a break and wiping his brow.

"Her scent's changed since she's been here."

Harley brought the hammer down too hard on the hot metal, and the sparks flew. "It's her."

Ryan heaved on the bellows again. "Then what are you waiting for? She's at the house and you're always here. It's not exactly conducive to a burgeoning relationship."

Harley let the hammer bang down on the metal, flattening and shaping it. When the rod cooled a little, he shoved it back into the coals and pulled out the other piece. "She gets a month to relax. A month to not worry about what I want from her. After..."

Ryan was so shocked he forgot to pull on the bellows. "Christ," he marveled, "I never expected you to be nice."

Harley shot him a dark look and nodded toward the pull. "It's the only freedom she'll have. After I take her, she'll be lucky to get five feet from me."

Ryan laughed and pulled.

...

Abbie felt she understood what a true home was supposed to be. After being in Killian's for several weeks, she finally grasped the entire concept, comfort, familiarity, and peacefulness. It was all part of what made it so nice. Maybe that was why she appreciated it so much she'd never been in such a relaxed atmosphere before.

As a child, she'd lived in a nice house, but it had been anything but comforting. With her parents arguing all the time, her mother harping, and the farm always there requiring time and attention from her father, the house was more a place of perpetual discontent. Then, after her parents divorced, she'd never been able to settle enough in either of their homes, feeling as if she didn't truly belong in either one.

But here, it was different. There was no one telling her to sit up straight or complaining when she got dirty or tore a shirt, and because of that, she was able to relax, help Killian with meals when she wanted, Ryan with the horses, and spend hours upon hours in the studio. Sometimes Killian was there with her, and sometimes he wasn't. It didn't seem to matter at all one way or the other since they worked well with each other, neither one of them intruding on the other's concentration. Plus, then she got to see him create.

She even became accustomed to the almost constant night, the snow, and the cold and enjoyed the extremes of winter. There was something savage about it, but beautiful, too.

She laughed more in the month with them than in the last eight years of her life. Ryan especially seemed intent on making her giggle constantly whispering raunchy jokes in her ear, then smiling innocently when Killian or Harley caught him.

Even dinner was completely different from what she was used to. It was a fun, informal event. Harley often came to the table late. Killian never seemed bothered one way or the other about it, and generally started the meal without him, smiling at his son when he finally made it, dishing out food as if nothing was wrong. And to him, there was nothing wrong. That was perhaps what endeared him so much to her. He loved his children without trying to change them.

She even felt she was getting used to Harley's dark ways, even if it wasn't easy. He was large and scary, and sometimes he made her breathless, which she couldn't quite understand. He didn't like her much she figured that out after two weeks. It was in his eyes and the way he avoided talking to her. It was hard to take at first, but finally, she just shrugged it away. It wasn't that difficult.

He spent his days out in his shop, pounding on hot metal and making swords, which she learned from Killian were often purchased by serious collectors and museums, and even occasionally used in movies. As it turned out, she rarely saw him accept during the dinner meal, and then she had Killian and Ryan to act as buffers.

Her mother was the only dark spot in her new life, but it wasn't a new problem. She had called her a few days after going to the pub. After listening to her mother's ranting, she chastised herself for even bothering to try and explain her situation.

"Do you know what people are saying?" her mother screeched.

"No," she replied woodenly, clenching her hand around the phone. Killian looked at her from the counter where he was rolling pie crust, clearly concerned.

"Jane Green is saying you went off with a boyfriend because you're pregnant."

She winced, knowing her mother's reaction to that one. She had been so afraid of her daughter becoming a teen pregnancy statistic, she hadn't even allowed her to date in high school.

She listened for another few minutes, making no comment as her mother ordered, prodded, begged, and yelled, insisting she come home and return to the hospital.

She finally couldn't take anymore and interrupted. "I love you, Mom." She hung up the phone.

She woke later than usual one morning, several weeks later. She went to the kitchen, and Ryan was wolfing down a huge breakfast. She helped herself to cereal and joined him at the table.

"Good morning." She carefully added milk, making sure not to splash.

"Is it?" he mumbled.

"What's wrong with you?" She scowled at him and set the carton down a little more forcefully than necessary.

"Shitty night." He shoved more food in his mouth and chewed viciously. She paused with her spoon just about to dip into her bowl. "I'm sorry. Is there anything I can do?"

His eyes slid over her for a second before returning to his plate. "No."

His tone rankled. Taking a deep breath, she decided the day would be best spent in the studio, preferably alone.

When she came downstairs hours later, loud voices coming from the kitchen. She stepped carefully down the stairs, keeping off the sections that squeaked and listened. For once, they were speaking in English.

"You can't stay, Harley. You're taking over. I guarantee, boy, Theron will have convinced someone else to bring a challenge. And I'd expect more than one."

"She's my responsibility, Harley. Not Ryan's."

"He likes her and volunteered, Harley, don't act like a fool when we're here to help you. She'll be fine."

Harley retorted with something too low and guttural for her to catch. She stepped down a few more steps and waited. The conversation stopped for a second, then returned to Gaelic.

Sighing, she gave up and tromped down the rest of the steps. She didn't bother trying to be silent dragged her feet and tapped on the walls as she headed for the kitchen, just to be irritating. It was uncanny how well they could hear, and inconvenient. The tiniest little squeak of a floorboard and they switched to Gaelic. Any hope to eavesdrop was completely swept away. Killian stood at the stove wearing a black apron around his waist. His eyes snapped to her briefly before returning to Harley, who looked perfectly calm, although his eyes glittered with emotion.

Deciding that directness was the right approach, she said, "Don't worry about me. Go ahead about your business. If the three of you want to go hang out and do whatever," she gave a little shrug, "that's fine. I don't need a babysitter."

She tried to keep her voice light and unconcerned. Killian looked slightly worried, but he didn't interrupt other than to pull open the oven and take out a pan of brownies. Harley said something in Gaelic to him. She couldn't tell what it was, but it didn't sound polite. Killian watched absently as the younger man turned and left.

"What's his problem?" she asked, eyeing the brownies. The smell was divine.

"He worries."

She selected one carefully and bit into it, humming with pleasure as she licked the chocolate off her fingers. "Is that why he doesn't like me? Because he thinks I'm his responsibility, and therefore a burden?"

Killian stared at her in shock. "Where did you get that idea?"

She shrugged and took another bite. "It's okay. It bothered me at first, but I'm okay with it now. Everyone doesn't have to like me, and I get that. But I'm not his responsibility, Killian. I can take care of myself, mostly. You guys don't have to worry about going out together and leaving me alone. I'll be fine."

He didn't say anything as he stared at her and went back to removing brownies, shaking his head slightly and muttering something like, "Stupid foolish boy."

"So, when are you guys going out?"

"Wednesday. We'll leave about noon and be back late."

It wasn't the first time she'd heard of men doing an all-night poker party or some other similarly manly activity. "Okay. Like I said," she smiled at him and took another cookie, "I'm a big girl. I can entertain myself for a few hours."

"I know."

Harley didn't come to dinner that night. She almost asked, but the expression on Killian's face said he wasn't in the mood for questions. She let it go and hurried through the meal.

Ryan was equally tense. He hadn't made any crude jokes in two days, and she was starting to worry about it. They all acted like they were going to an execution rather than a guy's night out. It was strange. Wednesday rolled around, and she was relieved for no other reason than to get it over with. She was tired of the side glances from Killian, and the silence from Ryan. It was unlike them and made her uncomfortable as if she were ruining their previously easy existence.

She got up early, went to the studio, and started working with a pen and ink the day before and liked the results. Charcoals were still her favorite, but the clean line of the pen was a nice change.

At 10:00, she cleaned up and headed downstairs, ready to reinforce Killian's faith in her.

"I think it's going to—" She stopped speaking and inhaled sharply. "Sorry. I thought you were Killian."

Harley stood in the kitchen, leaning back against the sink with his head bowed. His eyes lasered in on her, heavy and cold, and for the first time, she saw true emotion behind them, although she had no idea what it was. It was too cold to be angry, but too hot to be disliked. When she moved a step back, he traced it, like an animal watching prey and getting ready to pounce.

"I want to speak with you for a minute."

She stared at him, not quite sure she'd heard him right or heard him at all, to be exact. He hadn't said five words to her in two weeks. What could he possibly need to speak about now?

Prepared to take some type of criticism, she nodded.

He moved closer, until he was just a few inches away, which forced her to tilt her head back, so she could look him in the eyes. She wanted to take a step back but didn't. He would probably move forward again, anyway.

"You know we're leaving soon."

She nodded. "Yes. And it's fine. I'm okay by myself."

His jaw clamped for a moment. She felt sure he was going to say something scathing, but he didn't.

"Is that all?" she urged, wanting to get away. She felt that she was growing stronger and braver every day. But, she wasn't strong enough or brave enough to deal with Harley for any length of time. Short amounts of time, preferably under fifteen minutes, yes. Much longer than that, and she was out of luck. He was too imposing.

His jaw clamped for a moment. She felt sure he was going to say something scathing, but he didn't.

"Is that all?" she urged, wanting to get away. She felt that she was growing stronger and braver every day. But, she wasn't strong enough or brave enough to deal with Eben for any length of time. Short amounts of time, preferably under fifteen minutes, yes. Much longer than that, and she was out of luck. He was too imposing.

"No." He took a deep breath and held it like he was trying to smell something. She frowned at the action, thinking it strange.

"Don't leave the house after we're gone, for any reason. Don't unlock the door for anyone. There's an emergency number by the phone. If anything happens, call it immediately. The person who answers will get us a message. Do you understand?"

"I'm not a ch—" She snapped her mouth shut. After a minute, she just nodded.

"We'll leave in an hour." He turned away from her and left the kitchen. She watched him go and scowled. Then stuck her tongue out at his retreating form, she wasn't that much trouble.

CHAPTER 10

In all honesty, she was looking forward to them leaving. She was used to solitude and enjoyed it. It was one of the reasons why she liked the studio so much. It was quiet and peaceful, and even when Killian was there with her, she hardly noticed because both of them were so wrapped up in their work. The house would be all hers and she was ready for it. She had chocolate, chips, and sodas. All that was required was entertainment, and that was easy since the movie collection stored in the entertainment center was large enough to rival Netflix. There were hundreds of movies, of every category, and it wasn't long before she had several she thought interesting. The three men entered the room while she went through the last drawer, muttering about "stupid Ben Affleck." She looked up and saw them standing by the door. Ryan carried a duffel bag, all three were in their jackets.

"Leaving?" she asked, getting up from the floor.

"It's that time," Killian replied. "You won't be bored, will you?"

"God, no. There are plenty of things to do here. Don't worry about it and have a good time." She hugged him and smiled reassuringly. Ryan gave her a little wave and headed out the door, followed closely by Killian. Harley stayed and stared at her, hard.

She raised her brows and pursed her lips, wondering what else he wanted to harp about. Folding her arms over her chest, she said, "I think they're waiting."

His mouth tightened. "Remember," he ordered, stepping toward the door. "No one comes in."

She nodded and watched as he closed the door behind him. The lock sounded like a gunshot in the empty house.

Hours later, the night was cold and windy. Snow fell heavily, but she hardly even noticed. Keanu Reeves called to her on-screen, kicking major ass. Before that, she'd had Rusell Crowe in Gladiator and before that, Top Gun, with Tom Cruise. All in all, she thought it was a very successful night.

She was in the middle of switching DVDs when a sharp, pained cry broke the night, the sound alone enough to make her wince and run to the window. The creature cried again, this time louder and more desperate. She pushed the curtain away and searched, looking for any sign of movement.

There was another scream of pain before she saw anything, and what she did see infuriated and flooded her with such rage she couldn't do anything to stop it. Without a thought, she left the window and ran to the front door, unlocking and yanking it open with more anger than she'd experienced in the last nine years. She didn't think to grab a jacket as she marched out into the night, walking into the cold with nothing more than her blind fury. She marched around to the side of the house, stopping when she spotted the man walking around the wounded creature. The animal was completely in shadows, hidden by the overhanging boughs of the trees, but she knew the sound of a wolf when she heard it.

"What do you think you're doing?" she yelled. She marched closer to them, not stopping until she had a clear view of the man's face. She memorized it, determined to give Killian a detailed description of the poacher. "This is private property. You're trespassing and better leave now. The cops are on their way." She wasn't sure where the lie came from, but it sounded good.

He was medium height, with what seemed like a slightly paunchy build, although she couldn't tell because of his heavy winter clothing. He raised his face from the animal and smiled at her, his thick lips spreading into a creepy smile. "There you are pretty girl."

He stepped away from the wolf and walked toward her. She had a view of the creature's back, covered in a thick, pale pelt. It didn't move.

"There's someone who wants to meet you, pretty girl."

She jerked her attention back to the man, and for the first time felt a frisson of alarm run up her spine. She'd been fueled by anger when she'd seen the poacher, but now, with him approaching her in such a threatening manner the word stupid ran through her mind on a banner.

"What would a pretty little piece like you be doing in this place, huh?" He stopped a few feet from her, and she smelled the heavy odor of onion on his breath.

"Especially with stupid dogs like this?"

Cautiously, she took a step back, and then another. "Leave. The cops are going to be here any minute." The wind whined, blowing her hair into her face. He sniffed at her and smiled wider, revealing crooked, yellow teeth.

"Liar. I can smell it all over you. Plus," his smile widened, "I cut the phone line. Won't be getting no calls out of this place for a while." Suddenly, his smile disappeared, and he licked his lips in a predatory manner. "I'm going to taste you, pretty girl. After I've had my fill, Theron can have you. What do you say to that?"

Abbie's breath froze in her chest. The snow was coming heavily, hitting her skin like tiny little darts. She exhaled slowly, everything stilled, and a second later, turned and ran, so quickly that she almost slipped into the snow. Her heart raced, thumping heavily in her chest as she rushed for the front door. She could see the door, so close. It was safe. All she had to do was get in and lock it. She heard him breathing heavily behind her for a second before he grabbed her and yanked her back. She went tumbling into the snow and his heavy body landed on top of her, smashing her into the cold, frozen ground.

She screamed and scratched at him. He slapped her hard, then again when she didn't stop struggling.

She blacked out in a daze for a minute. Everything spun around her crazily. The sky was a sheet of black velvet, tumbling in waves above her head. Occasionally, her attacker appeared in her vision, ripping at her clothes, and squeezing her flesh painfully. She gasped as he jerked at her pants and came back to herself. She was nearly nude, wearing only shreds of her clothes, lying in the frozen snow. Above her, he reached for his zipper and pulled down his pants. His cock flopped out, red, pointed, and dripping with pre-cum.

She tried to leap up and get away, but he was on her in a second. Viciously, he grabbed her by the back and flipped her around, slamming her back into the ground.

"You will stay still, slut!"

Tears ran down her face in hot streams. He was working his cock, trying to get closer to climaxing. At the same time, his other hand grasped her thigh, bruising her as he wrenched her legs apart.

With a last thought to survival, she kicked her leg up, hitting him in the balls. With a short cry, his eyes rolled up and he crumpled, both hands going to his groin. With a single glance, she scrambled away, crawling on her hands and knees for the woods, with no thought except to get away.

A streak flew past her, six and a half feet dark brown against the snow. It growled and snarled as it launched itself at her attacker. It growled low in its throat, and her breath froze she was staring at her nightmare again.

Through her haze of pain, she watched as the creature tore and ripped at the skin of the man. Her attacker was suddenly growling and changing before her, his bones and skin popping and reshaping, reminding her of too many horror movies. Hair sprouted all over his body as his clothes tore away until his form. *Werewolf.*

She stayed where she was, collapsed in the snow, unable to tear away from the horrible sight before her. The brown werewolf was already bleeding, already hurt. It flinched and screamed as the paler one aimed and bit down, tearing a large piece of flesh from its side.

Then it seemed to get a second wind, and seeing an opening, it went for its opponent's neck, pinning the paler werewolf to the ground. With a fatal shake of its head and a tearing of flesh, the paler wolf howled in pain, a small geyser of blood splashing across the snow and gurgling in its throat.

She lay still in the snow, watching the creature's death spasms. It died jerking and yelping, its legs twitching.

The other werewolf collapsed with a cry, its back arching in pain. Even in the dark, its blood was visible on the pristine snow.

She couldn't tell how much time passed as she huddled in the snow, that old and familiar numbness strong, making it possible for her to survive. Her shirt was in shreds, and her jeans were gone. She had to warm up or she'd die in the cold. Stumbling, she moved closer to the house, watching both forms cautiously, on guard for sudden movements.

She was close to the house when the brown form turned toward her, its clawed hand/paw reaching for her.

"Abbie," it groaned through vocal chords not meant to speak. She stilled, new fear flooding her bloodstream. With disbelief and horror, she crawled toward it. It couldn't be. "Ryan?"

Its huge head rolled, and foreign, feral eyes blinked at her, clouded with pain. Its mouth opened, revealing rows of jagged teeth as he gasped, "Call Killian, Abbie."

Her shivering suddenly became violent. Pressure exploded in her chest, demanding to be released.

Her cry broke the night, full of hurt and confusion.

The Ryan creature inched closer to her, and she scrambled back. Its lips lifted in a growl of warning. "Don't."

She cried silently with her arms wrapped around her chest. How could this be?

How could she not know?

"Abbie," he growled again, his voice weaker.

She sucked in her tears and looked around her. She was outside, nearly naked, and hurt. Feeling as if waking up from a long nap, she tried to get to her knees and immediately fell again.

"Go. Now."

She tried again, and fell again, sprawling even closer to him. For a second, she lay there, unable to move. "I don't think I can," she whispered.

"Get up!"

She scrambled away, fear giving her strength. The house was there, she could make it.

CHAPTER 11

Falling every few steps, she pushed herself to the door, agonizing and crying the entire time. When she finally touched the handle, she could hardly feel it, her fingers were so cold. She had to try three times before it opened properly, and she was able to pull her body inside. She locked the door immediately. She lay in the hallway, panting and crying until she was warm. She had no idea how long it took, and hardly even thought about it. Her mind was empty suddenly, giving her time to heat up before dealing with other issues. The numbness was still there, protecting her from the terror, and she let it take hold, thankful.

She stood up on shaky legs finally, slightly dazed. As if it were any other day, she glanced down at her body, seeing the bruising and blood. She studied it and then pushed it out of her mind, too. *Later.* She'd deal with it all later. Humming slightly, she walked to her room and pulled out sweatpants and a shirt. After getting dressed, she went and sat in the living room, shivering. And she waited. Her mind stayed pleasantly empty as she stared at the shelves of books. So many, all different colors. She could look at them forever and not get bored going over the differences. Maybe she would do that.

The clock struck midnight. She jerked her head up and stared out the window, as all those thoughts she didn't want poured into her head. Ryan was a werewolf, like the monster she saw the night her father died. He was a monster. She absorbed the information, trying to get a handle on everything. But it didn't feel right. Monsters were things that only destroyed and killed, with no thought to the pain they caused others.

She'd been alone with him, joked with him, laughed with him, and he'd never tried to hurt her. He hadn't even made a pass at her and liked all women, short, tall, thin, thick. He loved women.

And he was lying out there in the cold, bleeding and hurt. Possibly dying. Jerkily, with fresh tears running down her face, She stood up. Call Killian, he'd said. She could do that.

But when she got to the phone, there was no dial tone. Her attacker hadn't been lying about cutting the line.

With that avenue taken from her, she went to the door. If she helped him, she'd have to get him inside. He couldn't stay in the cold while hurt so badly. Knowing what she was going to do, she put on her boots and pushed the door open. He was exactly where she'd left him, covered with a light dusting of snow. He didn't move as she stepped close to him. Carefully, she kneeled next to him and with a shaking hand, reached out and laid it on his thick neck where his pulse would be if he were human.

He groaned. Scared, she jerked her hand back and stared down at him. His eyes slit open, revealing his canine eyes.

"Go," he groaned roughly.

Her breathing was too fast and froze in the frigid air, looking like little clouds. She wasn't sure if she'd be able to do it. But somewhere, she found the strength. "I can't lift you," she shivered. "You need to stand and hold onto me to get inside."

His claws scraped at the frozen snow as he realized what she was saying.

"Can you do that?" she asked, her voice quivering.

His muzzle moved in the dark. "Yes."

She reached out but stopped just shy of touching him. His body was covered in a thick pelt of brown fur. It got shorter on his stomach and around his cock, which was embarrassingly visible. His body was heavily muscled, but it wasn't human muscle, just as his altered bone structure was also foreign and had similarities to wild canines.

Taking a deep breath, she set her hands on his chest and moved them up to where his front legs/arms met at his shoulders. She tugged and brought him up to a half-reclining position. "Come on," she urged, grunting with strain. He snarled at her, but she held on, and together, they managed until he was sitting, with his awkwardly bent legs in front of him and his clawed hands wrapped around hers for support.

"Okay," she huffed. "I'm going to pull, and you have to stand. On the count of three."

He howled with pain when she got him up. His weight immediately crashed down on her, and she nearly fell over with it. He had a thick gash across one of his legs, and it bled freshly as he put weight on it. She also got a look at the wound on his side. The muscle across his ribs and stomach was torn, and strings of tissue hung loosely, dripping blood into his thick fur. The wounds bled sluggishly, but what shocked her was how some of the flesh was already knitting together at the top. Astonished, she realized he was already healing.

"Move!"

She forgot about his wound and concentrated on their most immediate threat, which was the cold. She walked awkwardly with his huge frame pressing down on her like a ton of bricks. He groaned and whined with nearly every step, clearly pained from his wounds.

They made it to the house finally. She had to reach for the door with one hand while she kept the other around Ryan's furred middle. Once the door was open, they limped inside.

They walked through the foyer and headed for the living room. Once there, Ryan released his grip and fell to the floor. She stared down at him in a daze, noting the blood covering his side and muzzle. In the dark, he could easily have been the creature that caused the crash.

Her legs gave out and she slid to the floor, leaning against the couch. Her eyes went over the creature's form, looking for any sign of Ryan. It was his eyes that reassured her, and she held that thought tight, repeating it again and again in her head.

CHAPTER 12

She woke up suddenly, her body screaming in pain. For some reason, her head felt like it was three times the normal size and filled with bricks. Large bricks.

"You look terrible."

She squinted in the dark and saw Ryan, lying on his stomach and slightly curled inward. In a flash, the night's events tumbled through her mind, and she groaned.

He was no longer covered in fur, but back to his normal form. A deep gash was still evident on his side, but it looked like it was days old, already covered in scabs and healing skin.

He was nude but didn't seem to be the least bit embarrassed. His eyes were open, they were plain green, just as she remembered.

"Harley's going to have my head when he comes back and sees you like this," he remarked tiredly. "Why the fuck didn't you call them?"

"Phone's out." She tried to sit up and cried out from the pain. For some reason, it felt like someone had taken a whip to her back. "Is that man," she choked over it for a second, "dead?"

"Yes." There was no apology in his eyes.

"Do I look that bad?" she whispered, lifting her hands. They were bruised, scratched, and shaking violently, so she shoved them down into her lap.

"You do. Plus, you're bleeding. I can smell it."

She flinched, thinking about that strange ability, which made her think about what he was. Hastily, she reached behind and pulled a blanket off the couch. She spread it across her body and huddled beneath it.

"Yeah," he drawled, "that'll make a difference. They'll never notice now."

"Shut up," she breathed.

They both fell silent, waiting. Killian had said they'd be back late; it was way past late.

The time crawled by, both tense and hurting, anxious for Killian's return. The clock struck 3:50, Ryan stiffened, and then Abbie heard the sound of the front door opening. Her head lolled against the couch cushion and her eyes closed. It was a relief to know help was coming.

"They're like you, aren't they?" she asked in a whisper.

"Yes," he replied, just as quietly.

It was a thought that should have frightened her. It did frighten her, especially Harley, but it also explained so many things.

There was no sound of running feet, but suddenly they were both there. Killian took one look and kneeled next to Ryan with a quiet, controlled, "Damn him to hell." Abbie couldn't tell who he was damning and wasn't in the mood to ask.

"Who?" Harley asked, standing over them. His voice was soft and detached, but his eyes were filled with blazing fire.

"It was Issac," Ryan said, his eyes closed and grimacing as he shifted slightly to allow Killian better access to his wounds. "Don't worry, I got him. He's behind the house."

"Is that a bullet in your back?" Killian asked, frowning at the hole in his skin.

"He shot me first." Ryan groaned, shuddering as he pressed his fingers to the area.

Harley stood over them, breathing far too slowly. He stared into Abbie's eyes as his changed, turning to that of a creature, a werewolf.

"We need to get the bullet out," Killian was saying, worry creasing his face.

"Don't worry about me right now. You need to check on Abs. She's bleeding."

Killian's eyes flew to her. "I thought that was you, Ryan."

Ryan winced and met Harley's eyes. "I failed you, Alpha. I was out for a little while after the bullet got me. He was trying to rape her."

"Was he?" Harley walked around the room, his pale, werewolf eyes moving from his brother to the huddled form of Abbie.

Ryan smiled in memory. "She kicked him in the balls. He was rolling around screaming when I got him."

"You saved me, Ryan," she argued weakly, trying to sit up against the sofa.

"He would have gotten me if not for you." And that was something for which she'd always be grateful.

Killian moved to her side; his face creased with worry. "I'm going to lift you onto the sofa, and then I need to remove your clothes, okay?"

She was already shaking her head. "He didn't do—" She sighed and tried again.

"He didn't finish. I just need help getting up and then I'll be fine."

"I don't know." Killian looked at her worriedly.

"Really," she insisted in a whisper. "I'll be okay as long as I can get to a shower."

Sensing that Killian was going to argue with her, she pushed herself up, hissing from the pain. Places she hadn't realized were hurt suddenly stood up and shouted with pain.

Especially her ribs, which she couldn't figure out at all. She took another deep breath and pushed until she was on her feet. She wobbled a bit before stabilizing herself with a firm hand on the couch.

"I want you to take a sedative before you take a shower," he ordered, standing and taking her arm, leading her from the room. "Then you'll sleep and hopefully escape without any nightmares."

She nodded and let him help her from the room. At the doorway, she turned and looked down at Ryan. "Thank you."

He smiled at her weakly. "My pleasure, duchess. Now, let Killian take care of you before he has a conniption fit."

Ryan waited until they were gone before questioning Harley. "How many challenged you?"

"Four."

"Deaths?"

His eyes slid to his brother. "Three."

He'd been injured. Ryan could see the cuts from claws across his cheek, and he could smell the fresh blood on him, even though he'd showered. It didn't matter. He'd be healed in two days anyway, the wounds no more than a memory.

"What happened to Harley?" she asked as Killian helped her sit on the toilet. "How'd he get those wounds on his face?"

He turned the shower on and adjusted the temperature. "As you've figured out, we're not exactly human. Harley has taken my place as Lead Alpha of the pack, and he had challengers."

Challengers. Abbie knew he wasn't talking about chess. "Did he win?"

"Sweetheart, Harley doesn't know how to lose." He pulled the curtain closed and turned to her; his face lined with worry. "Do you need help?"

She shook her head. The last thing she wanted was someone taking her clothes away. "I'm fine."

"Just shout if you need anything. I'll hear you."

He closed the door on his way out, and she was finally alone. The water burned when she first got in. After she got used to it, she scrubbed her body furiously, so hard she was red when she got out, but she needed to clean that man's touch from her body.

After slipping on a heavy set of pajamas, a gift from Killian, she slid into bed, feeling the effects of the sedative. Her eyes drooped and she let sleep take over.

CHAPTER 13

Abbie woke up early, feeling groggy from the pills and achy all over. She took another shower and examined her body in detail. Every inch seemed covered in a bruise or scrape and each one hurt. Her face was a disaster, but her back gave her the most problem. It burned every time she moved her arms.

"I think there's something wrong with my back," she told Killian after finding him in the kitchen. He looked worn and tired, and fifteen years older than usual. He nodded and set his coffee cup aside. "You'll need to remove your shirt," he said carefully.

Her heart thumped noisily in her chest. Turning, she hesitantly pulled her shirt off and held it against her chest. With her ribs and back hurt, she hadn't bothered with a bra.

She didn't hear Kilian step close, but suddenly he was touching her, his fingers gentle as he felt the tender areas. Even so, it was agonizing, especially when he pulled at the edges of the wound.

"That son of a bitch," he murmured finally, stepping away from her.

"Well?" she asked, turning to him.

"You saw him change, didn't you?" He stood back and stared at the pale expanse of skin revealed to him, crisscrossed with multiple furrows from sharp claws. She nodded. "When Ryan knocked him down, he changed."

"Abbie," Killian said softly, "he was partially changed when he hurt you. He ripped your back up pretty well with his claws."

She paled and gulped. Her voice came out wavering and weak. "Am I going to be like you now?"

He suddenly looked offended. "It's not a communicable disease, Abbie. We're a different species, not a virus. There's nothing that could happen that would change you and make you Were."

"Not even if I was bitten by one of you?"

He snorted. "Of course not. But," he held up a finger, "the wounds need to be cleaned and disinfected. And you could probably use some stitches."

Her breath whooshed out in relief. "I don't care. Do whatever." She smiled and wilted against the kitchen counter, feeling a weight had been removed from her shoulders. *Thank God!*

Killian patted her on the head and went to get his supplies.

Thirty minutes later, she was thankful for the local he'd given her and not smiling. She'd had stitches once before when she was eleven. A new bike from her father resulted in a deep cut on her chin along with her mother's never-ending wailing and complaining about scars. She did have the scar, but that emergency room visit, where her father had held her on his lap the entire time, was one of her fondest memories. He'd made her laugh even when the doctor came near with the needle. She winced and sucked in a breath, returning to the present when she felt Killian jab the needle through her skin and pull the threads. "Ow."

"Sorry, dear. Just another few I'm quite good at this, you know. Between the two boys, I've had quite a lot of practice."

"What, you guys don't like hospitals? There all sorts of funny stuff in your blood that would raise the proverbial red flag?" She shifted slightly in the chair and felt the tug of the thread again.

Killian's fingers moved nimbly against her back. "We don't exactly have a local emergency room around here. We're a bit far out for that. And since we do keep our existence unknown among the humans, obviously it's quite a bit easier to do without putting evidence in the hands of those who would most like to know. Scientists, doctors. That type. Wouldn't you agree?"

"Why do you do that?" she asked curiously. "The hiding thing, I mean?"

"There was a time, just hundreds of years ago when our kind was unfairly persecuted. Along with others, I might add. Our numbers decreased substantially. It's safer for us this way. We blend well with humans."

He snipped the last of the thread and set the needle aside. "You'll need to be careful not to pull it," he ordered, taking out a stack of gauze pads and tape and covering the worst of the wounds. "We can remove the stitches in a week and a half, and then you should heal as good as new."

She nodded. She slipped off the stool, her shirt still over her chest, and turned to question him about showers. Instead, she saw Harley standing in the doorway, and her questions died in her throat, forgotten. She immediately flushed and turned her back to him. "Do you mind?" She jerked her shirt over her head and shoved her arms through, trying to hide as much as she could manage.

Killian lifted his head from his medicine supply bag but said nothing. Harley left the doorway and walked into the kitchen, his body relaxed and flowing with the movement. "I told you to stay in the house."

With all her parts covered, she turned around and glared, not bothering to hide her irritation. "If I hadn't, Ryan could very easily have died."

"I gave you an order, Abbie." he said softly, leaning down so she couldn't avoid him. "And you agreed to follow it."

"I'm not your responsibility." She folded her arms over her chest and moved her eyes to the refrigerator. It wasn't towering over her angrily, so it was a big improvement over Harley. "And I'm not a child." She looked over at Killian, a slightly worried expression on his face. "Tell him."

But Killian only shrugged. "He is Alpha, Abbie. By that alone, you are his responsibility."

"Traitor," she muttered.

He smiled and left the kitchen, his supplies in hand.

Harley moved in front of her and again filled her line of vision. He was so still and silent it was alarming. He leaned in, his mouth so close to her ear she felt the warmth of his breath. "You're wrong," he whispered.

His response only served to increase her ire. "I'm twenty-three years old," she spat at him, glaring because she shouldn't have to deal with him. "I'm smart and capable, and I don't need anyone else telling me what to do! I'm sick of that shit."

He straightened and backed up until he was leaning almost lazily against the counter, his arms crossed over his chest and his head lowered slightly, staring at her from under his brow.

"You don't know what you're doing, little girl."

Feeling mutinous, Abbie tossed her hair over her shoulder and flipped up her middle finger. "Kiss my ass. I'm out of here."

She was all prepared to stomp off from her first honest-to-God fight, with him, no less, gloriously triumphant. And she would have, if he hadn't grabbed her and dragged her back, anchoring her back gently against his chest.

"What are you doing?" She pulled away or tried to, and didn't budge an inch. He growled. She stilled her struggles the moment the animal sound came from his chest. She'd almost forgotten and wanted to kick herself for it. She had to remember they weren't human, weren't even close. They were werewolves, monsters, known to kill and destroy without a thought, even if none of them had hurt her.

"I want to leave," she said stiffly.

His arms tightened around her, pulling her lower body tighter against him.

"Where's the fear, Abbie?" he asked in his crisply accented voice. "You should be scared, babe because you're not going to like this one bit."

She stiffened against him, and suddenly her blood ran cold. "Don't hurt me."

He smiled against her hair, inhaling her scent deeply. "I'd never. That's not what I want from you."

She looked over her shoulder at him and shuddered. He was so close, close enough to see the way his eyes were liquid green and changing, close enough to see the fine lines in his tanned skin, and close enough to see the slight points of his canines when he spoke.

"I don't think my disobeying you warrant this type of punishment. Can't you pretend I'm sorry and go on your way?"

He smiled, and it was devastating. Devilish. Wicked. Sexy. "Don't you want to know why I chose you? Chose to take you from the hospital?"

She shook her head. "No. Not at all."

He ignored her refusal and continued, a bitter smile tingeing his words with resentment. "Ryan was locked up there, caught in a park when the moon was nearly full. He found your drawing, and I needed to see you, to know if you were a threat to my people. And you are, Abbie."

She remained silent against him, completely unmoving in his arms but her heart going a hundred miles an hour. It was beating so hard she could feel the pulses in her neck. "I'm not a threat. I promise I won't tell anyone."

"But you already did." Languidly, he splayed his palm across her stomach, kneading her flesh gently, and it only made her nervousness worse. She wanted to wiggle away from it and did for a second but stopped when she felt the large bulge at her back, hard and insistent in his jeans. "Um, Harley..."

His voice dropped an octave. "You told your mother, doctors, everyone. You even drew pictures to show them, and that I can't have. My people's lives depend on secrecy, and you were destroying that."

She began panting as she realized what he was saying. "So, you're going to kill me?"

"I wish I could," he murmured, lowering his mouth to the side of her neck, letting his lips brush her soft skin in a small kiss. She shivered in reaction, and he smiled. "I wanted to, but there's another problem."

She waited on tenterhooks, wanting him to finish, but he just stood behind her, his hand lowering gradually over her tummy. His hips arched against her, and he groaned, making her twitch in his grasp.

"What are you doing?" she whispered harshly, her fear dropping back for a minute as she tried to figure him out. He looked like an axe murderer, all dark and dangerous. "Harley..."

His mouth stayed against her skin. "I want you, badly. I wanted to fuck you the second I saw you in the hospital. You were sick and weak, and I still wanted you, even then."

Her eyes widened in shock and her knees almost gave out. Her head snapped around. "You don't even like me!" she hissed. "You can't stand even being in the same room with me!" It couldn't be. It made no sense! She tried to turn her body, and he let her, although he still kept her pressed against him. Facing him, she shook her head slowly. "What's wrong with you?"

He took her hand in his and jerked it down his body, pushing her palm flat against the thick ridge in his jeans and holding it there. She tried to tug away but he held her firm. He spoke through clenched teeth, his voice deep and lethal. "I get hard every time I'm near you, Abbie and it hurts."

She shook her head again, not wanting to believe him. "So, what? You're mean to me? You're rude? Harley, people don't do that!"

"It's not easy for me," he bit out.

She clamped her mouth shut, her eyes narrowing slightly. It wasn't an answer. It was an excuse and a bad one. Finally, she asked, "What do you expect of me?"

He dropped her hand and let his palms rest on her hips, tucking her right against his swollen flesh. Gently, he rolled his hips and moaned at the sweet agony of it.

"You're mine, Abbie," he growled, letting his head fall toward her as he manipulated her body. "Ryan and Killian know, my pack knows, and I know. You are mine."

He punctuated his words with a hard pull of her hips, thrusting in time with them. Her breath stopped in her lungs with the movement. A coil of heat like nothing she'd felt before pooled low in her groin, and she wanted it to stop, needed it to stop.

"So, you want me to have sex with you."

His dark hair rested against his forehead, black and wavy, so thick she wanted to run her hands through it. "Not sex, Abbie. I want to fuck. Hard, soft, any way I can. I want to lick you everywhere. I want your lips around my cock. I want it all."

His words made the heat worse. It built in her and mixed with the fear, sending little waves through her body. Her legs were weak, and her breasts ached. Her nipples felt like small, burning points. She gulped for breath and looked at him steadily.

"What if I don't want any of that?"

His smile was mocking. "I can smell your arousal. You can't lie to me."

"Oh God." Blood flooded her face in embarrassment. "I need to go. Please let me go."

"You disobeyed me," he whispered against her ear. His tongue darted out and swiped against her lobe, the motion so quick she wasn't quite sure she'd even felt it. "You destroyed any trust we were building, and you will pay for that."

His arms loosened. Panicked, she darted away and leaned against the wall, her chest rising and falling rapidly. As she watched him, he reached down and adjusted the large bulge of his cock within his jeans. He gave it a firm caress before walking around the counter and pulling a bottle of water from the fridge. He swallowed and she watched the thick line of his throat, saw his muscles flex.

His eyes blazed, and she realized how angry he was. He was dangerous, vengeful, and just plain pissed. "I'm moving your things into my rooms. You'll spend your nights there, in my bed. I want your scent thick there, Abbie."

She looked away from him, needing to focus on something inanimate. She picked the basket of fruit, arranged artfully by Killian just that morning. "Like I said," she breathed, trying to keep her voice steady and methodical, "I'm not your responsibility, and I don't belong to you. If you'll excuse me…" She stepped from the room, every muscle shivering and twitching. She was terrified. At least, she hoped that's what it was.

CHAPTER 14

Killian looked up from his book when he heard Abbie exit the kitchen. She went right past and didn't even see him.

When Harley followed a minute later, he stared in the direction she had gone. He didn't look pleased.

Killian asked, "Did you tell her?"

"No."

He sighed and laid his book aside. "Are you going to?"

Harley turned and came into the living room. He sat in the chair across from him and leaned forward, his elbows on his knees and his head bowed. He sighed and said quietly, "No."

"She has to know she's your mate."

His head rose. He stared at Killian, his eyes filled with angst, guilt, and determined ruthlessness. "Not until I've had her."

He shook his head. "Harley—"

"She'll run from me," he said sharply, angrily. "If I tell her before, she'll try and leave me."

"She may try that anyway," he said simply, but he gave up and went back to his book. "Just be honest, Harley. You'll gain more from that than from withholding the truth."

"I'll try," was all he said.

Abbie hid out in the barn. It seemed like the safest place; she figured the horses would give her the heads-up if he tried to corner her there. Ryan was already busy feeding the horses. He moved stiffly, especially when using his right arm.

"How are you feeling?" she asked, closing the door firmly behind her. Three horses raised their heads in their stalls, saw her, and went back to eating contentedly.

He leaned on the pitchfork he was using and studied her. "Christ, I'm fine. How the fuck are you? You look like hell."

She smiled and shrugged. "Killian gave me an ibuprofen, and that helped with the swelling. We did stitches this morning, but otherwise, I'm okay." She shrugged again, the resulting pull of the stitches reminding her to be careful. He shook his head and went back slowly to cleaning stalls. "I'm surprised Harley let you out of the house like that. Issac is lucky he's dead. Harley would have ripped his spine out and skinned him alive."

Somehow, Abbie didn't think he was teasing. "I kind of left the house without telling. I needed to get out."

He looked over at her, one eyebrow raised. "He's going to kick your ass when he finds you." He tossed a forkful of soiled straw toward the wheelbarrow, then halted for a minute. "You need to be careful with him, Abs. He's not like the rest of us."

She studied her hands carefully, noticing the jagged edges of her nails. "Do you mean like a human, or like what you guys are?"

"We're Weres. Not monsters or werewolves, but Weres, and judging by the pictures you've drawn, you've seen at least one of us before. Not many of us would do what Issac did to you."

"What's wrong with werewolf?"

He narrowed his eyes at her. "Would you like to be named after some silly creature that has no sense or intelligence, and seems to always chase after the pretty, vapid girl and get nailed with a silver bullet, which by the way doesn't work at all. Have you seen any of the movies, or read the stories? Each one of them makes us either into a cannibalistic beast, or a paranoid freak covered in lots of hair, with a perpetual hardon."

"So, you call yourselves Weres," she intoned. "Isn't it just semantics?"

He raked fresh straw into the stall as he continued. "So, what if it is? We are what we are, and we'll be called what we want to be called. We're pretty simple creatures, Abs. We like a good hunt, a good run, and a good fuck. In our pelts, we're likely to chase you down if you run, but after that, you'd probably be left alone, if a little bruised. It's the animal instinct in us so remember that if you're faced with one of us after the change. We're like humans in a lot of ways, love. There are bad Weres, just as there are bad people."

"Which one is Harley?"

He looked over at her, his eyes darkening slightly. "He's a bit of both and that's what makes him so strong."

She groaned and dropped her head into her hands. "I'm in trouble, then."

Ryan smiled at her sadly. She was such a young, inexperienced woman. "Yeah, you are."

She made Ryan go to the house first and call the barn to make sure Harley was in his shop. He laughed at her, but she ignored him, more interested in avoiding another confrontation than anything else.

It wasn't that she wasn't interested in his offer because there was a part of her that definitely was. Actually, a large part. But what would she do once she was in his bed?

Her mother had accused her of being a slut from the time she had her first period. The last thing she wanted to do was prove her right.

She skipped dinner and spent the time in the studio drawing scenes of Ryan, his body reshaped into his Were form. She also sketched the man who'd attacked her, Issac, in the middle of his change, with his bones at awkward angles and his face frozen in pain.

When she went downstairs a few hours later, all was quiet. Killian read in his leather chair, now and then reaching over for the glass of cognac at his side. He didn't even look up when she came down the stairs.

She was more than ready for bed. Her jaw throbbed, her back ached all she wanted was her sanctuary of peace and sleep. *Lots of sleep.* When she got to her bedroom, her jaw flopped open. She couldn't even gasp or shriek as she stared at her empty room, devoid of even sheets and blankets.

"That bastard," she finally whispered. She rushed through the room, pulling open drawers and cabinets, each empty of her possessions. He'd even taken her shampoo from the shower.

She did a small twirl around the room. It was like it had never been hers. Not even a sock was left behind.

She stood in the room for several minutes fuming, unsure what to do, her hands clenching over and over again. She couldn't confront him, he'd have her hauled into his bed in a minute flat, and that wasn't something she was ready to tackle. She was best off avoiding him completely and handling the situation on her own. She said nothing to Killian as she crossed the living room and stole a towel from his bathroom, but his eyes twinkled as he followed her march through the living room, which only made her irritation worse. Just to be bitchy, she also picked up the blanket from the sofa, daring him to say anything.

She showered quickly, afraid Harley would barge in at any moment. When she was done, she wrapped herself in the stolen blanket and lay on the bare mattress. It felt strange and a little scratchy, but she clenched her jaw and made herself relax. She was getting stronger, and she refused to give in. Minutes later, she fell asleep with the image of Harley, shirtless, in her mind.

Killian wasn't surprised when Harley came downstairs after midnight, a scowl on his face.

"Where is she?"

He nodded his chin toward her room. "There. She snagged the blanket from the sofa." He smiled at the memory of Abbie stomping through the living room, her jaw set. Harley ran a hand over his hair, pushing it back from his forehead. He was shirtless but wore a loose pair of pajama bottoms that hung around his waist, hanging off his hipbones. He slept nude, but he was trying not to scare his human mate.

He sighed and scratched absently at his chest. "Hell, she's becoming more rebellious every day."

Killian flipped the page of his book, his eyes sparkling merrily. "She's comfortable, Harley. Probably for the first time in her life."

Harley turned toward her room and halted. His shoulders stiffened as he asked, "Am I wrong to want her so badly?"

Killian's book lowered as he too remembered what it was like, to find the woman that both parts wanted, the man and the beast, with equal measure. It was a need, violent and pure, but so strong it was frightening at times especially when it was for a human. "I don't know. I truly don't know, Harley."

A minute later Harley came through the living room, holding Abbie's blanket-wrapped form. She snuggled into his bare chest, completely oblivious to the tension she was creating.

"Good night," Harley murmured, going up the steps as silently as he'd come down.

"Good night," Killian whispered. "And sweet dreams."

CHAPTER 15

Abbie woke with a stretch and a happy sigh. Any night without nightmares was a blessing; she took each one as a gift. She'd feared that after the attack, her nightmares would return with a vengeance, the two memories merging to create an entirely new and terrifying version, but they hadn't. She blinked her eyes open and stared up at the ceiling. After a few seconds, she cocked her head and stared harder. Her room had no ceiling fan, yet one was above her head.

Sitting up slightly, she studied the room. It was larger than hers, with no bookshelves lining the walls. There were two windows both large and looking out onto the forest. A wooden rocking chair sat next to one of them, and a heavy wooden dresser next to the other. The bed that dominated the room was huge, with tall posts at each corner and thick, fluffy blankets covering it. Harley lay beside her, sprawled out on his stomach, all muscle, and tattoos.

They were thick and black, tribal in design. They ran around his upper arms and joined in the center of his back, running down his spine in a spiraled pattern, and eventually tapering midway down. She missed them in the forge because it was too dark and dingy.

"Dammit," she muttered, scrubbing her hand over her face, then wincing as she rubbed too hard across her jaw. She'd been so proud of herself, outwitting him at his own game. And in the end, it turned out she hadn't.

She moved the covers and prepared to slip out, the rustle sounding noisy in the quiet.

"Going somewhere?"

She halted with the sheets pulled up partially. Her eyes closed and she pursed her lips, sighing. "I'm getting up."

He rolled toward her, dragging the blankets and sheets with him. He rested against the pillows with his hands behind his head, his chest bare in the weak light. She immediately felt breathless.

"You slept well." His eyes traced the bare skin of her shoulders and back. With a huff, she leaned forward against her knees and wrapped her arms around them, hiding her nudity as best she could. "Where are my clothes?"

"Here," he rumbled. "Some in the closet and the rest in the dresser. Why are you nervous, Abbie?"

She shook her head over the quick subject change. "I wake up in a bed that's not mine, nude, with a man I don't know very well who until eighteen hours ago, I thought didn't like me very much. Gee, I wonder what could possibly make me nervous. I want my clothes."

He blinked lazily, his lashes looking impossibly dark against his green eyes. "Then go get them." A slow, lazy smile bloomed on his face, and she suddenly became breathless. Good lord, he was beautiful.

"I don't have anything on." She glanced down at her bare skin, flushing slightly. He rolled to his side and propped himself on his elbow. His other hand latched around her neck, pulling her face toward his. "I'll bargain with you," he whispered, his lips against her neck. "I'll get your robe, but I want something in return."

She shivered at the determination in his eyes and voice. "I'm not having sex with you for my robe," she said stiffly, trying to pull away from him. He laughed softly, the sound low and smooth. It soaked into her skin and left her hot and agitated.

"No, babe. That will come later after your stitches are out. What I want right now, is a kiss." He pressed a soft kiss to her neck and brushed his nose against her skin, the caress so soft she couldn't help her eyes close. "Will you do it?"

She opened her eyes and looked around the room again. No shirts or clothes were left on the floor or hanging from the doorknob, so she'd have to scramble until she found something she could throw on, which could take several minutes and be embarrassing. Dignity is everything when that's all you've got.

"How old are you?" she breathed, the question popping out of nowhere. He stopped moving against her for a second, his hand flexing around her neck. There was no seduction in his voice as he asked, "Why?"

She nervously shrugged and kept her eyes glued on the darkness of the far wall.

"I'm twenty-three. I was wondering because I think you're probably a lot older than me, and I'm not sure if this is such a good idea. The differences..." She shook her head slightly, rather dramatically, she thought, and cut off her rambling. The "a lot older" comment was harsh, but she was in trouble. This was a war, after all, and she needed to bring out the big guns.

"Do you think I'll let you go because you find my age unacceptable?" His eyes grew chilly as he stared at her, one eyebrow raised. "I won't, Abbie. "

She looked away from him.

"Now," he said, "answer me on our bargain."

She opened her mouth for a second and almost backed down just from the tinge of bitterness in his tone. But she was a new strong woman, learning new things and living a new life. She refused to give up the precious little bravery she possessed.

It came out soft and breathy, more from wariness than true fear. "How old are you, Harley?"

His jaw tensed and the temperature in the room seemed to drop ten degrees. She had to exercise restraint to keep from rubbing warmth into her arms. The tension was terrible in the silence, like waiting for a bomb to explode.

"Fuck it," he muttered, tugging her toward him, the movement angry. "I deserve this." And his mouth crashed down on hers.

He wasn't gentle as his lips opened and his tongue plunged into her mouth, petting and licking, determined to wring a response from her.

She gasped and pushed at his shoulders, but he didn't budge. Instead, he pulled her more tightly against him, rubbing her nude body against his chest. His hands softly traced her spine down to her ass and rolling her hips against his blanket-covered groin. He rolled to his back and pulled her on top of him. She was in a daze, not sure what to do, what she could do, but sure she didn't want it to stop. His mouth was magic, driving thoughts from her head and making her so wild she wasn't sure it was healthy. He growled and nipped at her, traced the interior of her mouth with his tongue, and forced her to give more. He pulled his mouth away, just enough to growl, "Put your tongue in my mouth, Abbie."

He dragged his tongue from her collarbone up her throat in little circles. She groaned and arched her neck, wanting more. At her jaw, he gave special attention to the bruises before returning to her mouth and plunging in. She responded in kind and tried to follow his movements.

Embarrassment wasn't even an option for her, he didn't give her any time for it to catch. She was too busy sucking on his tongue and licking over his bottom lip.

"Do you want me to stop?" he asked, panting heavily. His hands cupped her breasts, kneading and brushing against her nipples which seemed to send fire straight to her groin.

She rolled her head back and tried to think and breathe, but it was hard. Every movement he made against her was torture. It was like having a rubber band in her abdomen, pulled taught and just waiting to be released, and the tighter it went, the less air she was able to suck into her lungs.

"No," she breathed.

His hand drifted from her right breast, down over her stomach, and slid between her legs for just a minute. His finger rubbed gently on her clit, making her want to scream.

"Now you know how I am, every day, waiting for you," he growled, pressing a quick kiss to her forehead and rolling her carefully off him.

She lay on her side, panting and in need. He was stopping now? That son of a bitch. She was dying. She had to be because there was no other explanation for the heat that was racing through her body, burning her alive.

"That was cruel." She sat up in the bed. Glancing down, she jerked the blankets up, covering her breasts.

He stood in the room, completely nude and so beautiful it almost hurt to see him. His legs were long and smooth, thick with muscle at the hip and thigh. His stomach was corded and ridged, full of tension. He had no body hair, except what was on his head. But it was his cock that finally took her attention. It bobbed heavily in the cool air, the tip deep purple and shiny with his fluids, slightly bulbous compared to the thick length below. He was long and thick, the sight of it scared the lust right out of her.

His nose flared slightly, scenting her fear, and his eyes warmed slightly.

"It'll fit, Abbie. I promise."

"Are you sure? That doesn't look quite…normal." She winced.

"For a Were, it's normal."

He went to the bathroom and came out holding her robe. She extended her arm from the covers and took it from him, keeping her eyes politely downcast. "Thank you."

He stayed by her side and ignored her discomfort. His hand cupped her jaw and turned her face toward him. "I want you to look at me," he said darkly, his eyes pale and intense. "I need it, Abbie, just as I need to look at you."

"No. I don't think so."

He bent toward her. "Let me convince you." His mouth touched hers again, this time gently, coaxing her to respond with each thrust of his tongue. It took disgustingly little.

She moaned and dropped the robe, shuddering as his mouth went to her neck, sucking and biting at the soft skin there.

He pulled away finally, staring with satisfaction at the marks on her neck. He pulled the blankets from her body and picked up the robe, holding it out toward her.

"Come," he ordered roughly.

She shivered in the chilly morning air. Seeing no way to win, she slipped from the bed, her whole body flushed with embarrassment.

He held the robe open as she slid her arms in, then pulled her hair away as she knotted the tie at her waist.

"You're very lovely."

She shrugged and kept her back to him, wishing she could be modern and strong about this rather than embarrassed. Maybe she'd get there eventually. No doubt, he'd offer her assistance in the endeavor.

He turned her around and tilted her chin up. She refused to meet his eyes.

"I'll be in the forge. I'll see you tonight." Pressing a kiss to her forehead he went to the dresser, pulled out clothes, and dressed quickly. Just before he closed the door behind him, he turned back and bit out, "Thirty-three."

She stayed where she was for nearly ten minutes after he was gone. Then, with a sigh, she collapsed onto the bed and admitted to herself that she was in serious trouble. And why didn't that scare her quite as much as it should?

CHAPTER 16

She stayed busy the entire day. She volunteered to clean all the horse stalls herself, ignoring Ryan's arguments about her stitches. She needed the activity, desperately. It was either get drop-dead tired or lust all day after a man she wasn't even supposed to like.

After the stalls, she swept the barn and scrubbed water buckets. When everything was done in the barn, she moved onto the storage shed, rearranging, and organizing everything, throwing out old paint cans and boxes wet with frost and mold.

"What is she doing out there?" Killian asked Ryan, staring through the window at the old shed where all the activity was occurring. Ryan sighed and watched through the window as she rolled an ancient bicycle through the door, leaning it against the wall. "She's trying to forget about Harley."

"This should be interesting," he commented.

Ryan agreed wholeheartedly.

When she came in later, Killian didn't waste any time admonishing her.

"You tore your stitches," he complained heatedly, glaring at her from the kitchen. "I can smell the blood from here, Abbie."

"Like I care," she muttered, throwing her jacket down. He raised his eyebrows and folded his arms over his chest. "Come in here. I'll be with you in a minute."

She glowered but stomped over and hunkered down on a stool. Shaking his head, Killian went to retrieve his bag of medical supplies and came in to find her glaring at the sink.

She winced through the process of cleaning the wounds and reapplying bandages.

"It's your fault," he grumbled. "I don't have to re-stitch them, but you pulled the threads." He finished bandaging and taping everything and then stood back to admire his work.

"Since I can't trust you, you're going to have to stay in the house until this properly heals m'dear. I'm sorry, but you don't want the mess torn stitches can cause. It's a nasty business, and I'd like you to have as few scars as possible."

Killian watched as she hopped from the stool and clomped toward her room. A minute later, a loud "Damn it!" echoed through the first floor. Ryan came to the door of the kitchen and looked in. "What happened?"

Killian smiled as he tossed the pieces of bloody gauze into the trash. "She forgot he moved her things into his room."

Ryan laughed.

The next week went by too quickly for Abbie, mostly because she was so busy avoiding Harley. She kept to herself mostly in the studio, working on anything to keep her mind occupied. As he'd promised, Killian refused to let her go to the barn, or anywhere else unless she gave him a full report of her activities. It was irritating, but she didn't grumble about it, excusing his behavior as a byproduct of worry. She saw little of anyone, and she liked it that way. There was too much tension in the air, and it only gave her a stomachache. The only part of her day she was forced to interact with everyone was during dinner, and that was chaperoned, although it did little good. Harley wasn't shy about his lust and desires; they were there in his eyes for anyone to see.

To avoid more embarrassing confrontations, she fell asleep on the couch every night after dinner. She hoped that he'd leave her there for the night. When that didn't pan out, she took comfort that she slept through him gathering her up and taking her to his room. He got up early in the mornings too so that was an extra win.

With that major worry out of her hair, she devoted her extra time to the computer Killian had in his studio. It was a small laptop hooked up to a satellite. It was filled with graphics programs, word processing, and other office tools, but what interested her most was the Internet.

Although she certainly wouldn't admit it to anyone else, it bothered her that she hadn't finished high school. She felt stupid not having that little piece of paper, even though she knew that was silly. So, she looked up GED programs, online college courses, and vocational schools. In for a penny, in for a pound, and all that. Besides, she needed to be self-sufficient and independent, after all, she wouldn't be able to accept Killian's charity forever.

"You're thinking about something," Killian murmured, as he carefully snipped the stitches from her back.

She rolled her shoulders and winced as he pulled the threads out. "I was looking up stuff on getting my GED."

He paused and stared at her over her shoulder, a smile wreathing his face. "I think that would be marvelous. I'm sure I still have some of the materials from when Harley did his. They should be in the den somewhere." He frowned, "Or maybe the basement."

"Harley didn't finish school either?" she asked curiously.

"Dear," he said, finally finishing up and dabbing the small holes with alcohol. "He was a teen when I found him and hadn't attended school a day of his life. I couldn't see enrolling him in a normal school. He had difficulties adjusting to just having a home and wouldn't have fit at all well, so I hired him a tutor. When he was ready, he took the exams, and he passed." He smiled at her as he closed his supply bag and set it aside. "I'm surprised you didn't take the test in the hospital. Don't they encourage that sort of thing?"

She tugged her shirt down and stood in front of him awkwardly, trying to come up with a way to explain her situation without making herself appear stupid. "They did, but I had another problem. I don't read very well." She smiled uneasily. "And with the drugs and everything well, it was difficult."

135

He folded his arms across his chest. "Explain about the reading."

"I'm dyslexic. I've had problems all my life so." She shrugged again, at a loss. "Dad had it too. It drove mom nuts because she had to go over pageant speeches with me and read everything until I memorized it."

He tossed the soiled gauze in the trash and wiped the counter. "I think one of the pack members is a teacher. I'll ask him and see if he can help."

Her eyes widened in alarm. "Please don't do that. I'd like to keep it private if that's okay."

"Abbie," he sighed, exasperated. "These are very nice people. Any one of them would be pleased to help you in any way they could."

"Please," she begged softly, desperate. "I'm not ready to go for help yet. I'd like to try by myself for a little while."

His eyes were steady, letting her know he didn't like it. "You'll ask me for help if you need it," he said sternly, the picture of a concerned father. She nodded and breathed out a sigh of relief. "Absolutely."

Later, at dinner, Killian asked Harley, "Do you remember where your high-school equivalency materials are?"

"In the office, I think. Why?"

Abbie dropped her fork and wanted to melt under the table as Killian cavalierly replied, "Abbie wants to get hers, and I thought your materials might help her study."

Harley's eyes swiveled to her. She prayed for death.

"I'll find them," he promised.

They went out running after dinner. She raised her head from the couch to see Ryan and Harley at the door, both just wearing jeans.

"We'll be back later," Ryan called, giving her a little wave as he went through the door.

Harley only stared at her before ducking out, his eyes heated. She waited for a minute, letting the quiet close over her and Killian, who was reading beside the fire.

"Are they going to... change?"

"Yes." He flipped a page.

She watched a movie and for the first time in a week felt relaxed enough to enjoy herself. There was no thought of avoiding Harley's advances or ignoring her own feelings. She was able to just sit back and enjoy her movie with no concerns. Halfway through, a loud howl split the night. Killian raised his head, his eyes getting a faraway look as he stared through the window at the woods just beyond.

"Why don't you go out?" she questioned, the look of wanting in his eyes hitting her hard.

He smiled at her and raised his book again. "One of us needs to stay with you. Some out there will try to hurt you just to get to Harley."

She absently ran her fingers over the buttons of the remote, feeling the difference in texture between the smooth plastic and the rubber buttons. "Is that why that other man hurt me?"

He looked over at her. "We don't know. He was dead by the time we got home, remember?"

She pursed her lips, going over that night and wondering if she should ask the question flying through her head. After peeking a few glances at him, she finally did, making sure her voice stayed light and absent of worry. "Who's Jaxon?"

His book slid down again, but this time there was no mistaking the demand in his eyes. "Why do you ask?"

"You guys say his name a lot and I was just wondering." She stared at the carpet and hoped she sounded convincing enough.

Killian didn't relax and tilted his head to the side. "You're lying," he murmured. "I can smell it."

"Who is he?"

His eyes became just as cold as Harley's just before he went back to his book.

"He's a Were who thinks to challenge Harley for control of the pack."

She mulled over the information, chewing her lip in thought. Harley had told her everyone knew she belonged to him. Apparently, he wasn't kidding.

"Where did you really hear the name, Abbie?"

She could see how much he wanted the information, but it worried her. Ryan had killed Issac, protecting her from his attack. Jaxon, even if he'd convinced the other man to take her, hadn't done anything wrong, and she wasn't sure if she could live with his death on her hands, all because of something she possibly could have misinterpreted. "From you guys," she said finally. "Really."

His expression said he was skeptical. "I'm going to tell Harley you asked. He'll insist on questioning you," he warned.

Her heart plummeted but she didn't back down. "I'm not lying."

He smirked at his book, the hard look in his eyes finally dissipating. "Sure, you are, love."

She fell asleep with no difficulties but woke up just a few hours later, starved. She tiptoed downstairs, checking carefully to make sure there were no threatening, furry bodies prowling around. When she was sure the coast was clear, she went to the kitchen and started digging.

Killian had plenty of goodies in his cupboard, along with some stuff that was just gross. Duck liver pate? She'd rather carve out her eyeball. After careful consideration, she went with the chocolate, marshmallows, and graham crackers. She hadn't had a s'more in years, and they were suddenly calling her name. She weighed the advantages and disadvantages of both the microwave and the stove as heating options and settled on the stove so she could have a crispy, golden-brown marshmallow rather than just a melted one. In one of the drawers, she found a beat-up fork and stabbed her two marshmallows down on the tines firmly. Killian insisted on using real silver at meals, and she hated to use one of his pretty forks for heating her marshmallows on the stove, not sure how the silver would react to the gas stove's flame.

The first marshmallows went up in flames and became a sticky, charred mess. But the second set didn't do so badly, although it took a little bit of maneuvering to get all sides properly browned. Getting the marshmallows onto the graham proved equally as tricky, but she managed and only burned her finger once. She added the chocolate and gently pressed down with the other graham.

She took a bite and moaned in joy. Although it was a slightly juvenile treat, it was good, far better than something as simple as crackers, marshmallows, and chocolate had a right to be.

She was in the middle of roasting the next batch when the front door pushed open. Ryan came in, a sleepy smile on his face, followed closely by Harley. It took her a second to spot the difference in him. He was relaxed, his movements slow and lazy even, like a cat waking up from a long nap. The whole week he'd nearly hummed with pent-up energy, and now it was gone, leaving just him, lethargic and at ease.

They both turned toward her at the same time. "Marshmallow's burning," Ryan blurted.

She returned her attention to her roasting marshmallows, only to find them flaming.

"Damn it!" She pulled them away from the flame of the stove quickly and blew out the fire. A small trail of smoke rose from the charred lumps, heading right for the smoke alarm. "Shit!"

Grabbing the nearest towel, she started waving it through the air, biting her lip and praying. Please, please, please, don't go off! Not like this, not in front of him!

Ryan glanced sadly at the charred marshmallow. "Well, since there's no chance I'm eating that, I guess I can go to bed. Good luck." He smiled and winked at Harley before loping off toward the stairs.

CHAPTER 17

Abbie abandoned her towel, feeling relatively certain she'd made a big enough fool of herself. Plus, the alarms weren't blaring, which was the only thing going right for her. With her jaw clenched, she cleaned up the mess she'd just made and tried not to feel nervous with Harley watching her so intently. After throwing the other lumpy mess into the trash, she stabbed another set of marshmallows onto her fork and held it over the flames of the stove. She didn't take her eyes off them for a second.

"I take it you had a nice time out there." She pulled the marshmallows up and made sure everything was golden brown before turning off the stove. He leaned against the doorway of the kitchen, his head tilting as she slid the marshmallows off the tines and onto a graham cracker. Like a chef admiring her work, she gave them a little pat with the top graham, squishing them just slightly before sliding a piece of chocolate in between.

"You know," she said as she turned toward him, her s'more in hand, marshmallow oozing out from the crackers. "It's your fault the other one burned, which is why I'm not going to give you this one. That's your punishment." She took a big bite out of it and chewed thoughtfully. "The marshmallows wouldn't have burned at all if not for you." She popped the rest of it in her mouth and dusted off her hands. Excellent.

"Love," he stepped fully into the room and poked at her s'more supplies, "what is it you're eating?"

"A s'more." She chugged down half a glass of milk which she'd had on the counter, handy whenever eating anything with chocolate. When she set the glass aside, he was still looking at the marshmallow and crackers as if he didn't quite get it. "Please tell me you've had one."

"I haven't."

Which should have been impossible, except he hadn't grown up where she had. He was homeless until he was nearly an adult, she reminded herself. He'd probably nearly starved more than once and had to steal his clothes. Deprived—that's what he was.

Businesslike, she flipped the stove back on and reopened the bag of marshmallows. "This, I can fix."

She laid the two marshmallows out on the counter, got the pieces of graham cracker and the wedge of chocolate ready, and put everything down in order. "The proper way to do it is over a campfire or grill. However, a good stove will work in a pinch. Why don't you come and stand here, and I'll coach you on the proper way to roast marshmallows."

"There's a proper way?"

"Of course. You do it wrong and you have melted marshmallow all over." Her skin prickled as he moved closer. When she saw that he was smiling, her heart sped up.

"You're laughing at me."

He dutifully took the fork and marshmallows from her. "I like it when you're bossy," he said, his voice all deep and gravelly. "What is it I'm to do with this?"

"Put the marshmallows on the fork. But do it through the ends, so they don't slip off when they're melted. Let me tell you, there's nothing worse than trying to clean scorched marshmallow off the stove burner."

"Nothing worse, is there? Then I take it you've had the pleasure."

"My dad and I," she said, smiling a little over the memory. "We used to do this at the stove. We had more than one accident." Seeing he had the marshmallows mashed down on the tines of the fork a little more than necessary, she got back to the business of proper roasting. "Now, this is the tricky part. Since you've never experienced the absolute perfection of a good s'more, then we're sort of operating at a disadvantage. You may very well be one of those sick and twisted individuals who likes burned marshmallows. I know," she said, her hands raised, "it sounds impossible, but let me assure you there are people out there who prefer them quite charred. And there are more of them than you'd think."

He looked at his squashed marshmallows skeptically. "I think you give this too much thought."

"Probably but wait 'til you've tried it. Only then can you mock. Now, go ahead and hold that over the flames a little, but not too close, or we may as well dig that mess out of the trash and slap that on a cracker." While she had time, she went to the refrigerator and refilled the glass of milk.

She came back to the stove to find him staring at her quizzically, his marshmallows not even close to the flames. Slowly, his head lowered toward hers, and she knew he was going to kiss her. She didn't move a muscle, too entranced watching as he came closer and closer. She closed the last few inches herself and leaned up on her tiptoes to press her lips against his mouth. Slowly, carefully, she moved against him, letting her tongue come out and dance against the seam of his lips. His hand came up and gently cupped her jaw, tilting her head just so as he widened his mouth. When his tongue flicked between her lips, she clutched at him and felt that same familiar heat burst through her loins.

After a minute, he lifted his head, his tongue licking across her lips at the last second just before he pulled away. She leaned against him, her head resting against his chest as she fought to get her breath. His skin was all warm and smooth against her cheek, the muscle hard but not uncomfortable to lie against. She could even hear his heartbeat just below her ear.

"Marshmallows," she reminded him, lifting her head and staring at the stove.

"Remember?" She pulled him directly in front of the stove. His discarded fork was sitting on the counter. She grabbed it, shoved it into his hand, and moved his arm an appropriate distance from the flame. "See? Not too close, so it won't burn to a crisp."

He leaned down and kissed her again, quick, and hard, and then turned his attention to the marshmallows, his unoccupied arm curling around her waist and keeping her at his side.

"And how do you know when it's done?"

She breathed in his scent and sighed. He smelled lovely like the outdoors, all piney and manly. "Everything is golden brown. Generally, that means the center is done, as well. But be warned, it doesn't always work out that way."

The silence grew while he finished the marshmallows, but it wasn't uncomfortable, and she wondered idly why she'd been so nervous the last week. It was easy to be with him like this.

"Okay," she said, breaking the quiet. "You're done. Now you have to slide everything off the fork without burning yourself yet still manage to get everything on the square of the cracker."

Almost so easily it was disgusting, he slid everything off, using the top cracker to direct the flow of the marshmallows. When he had it perfect, he looked up, his eyebrows raised. "Chocolate?"

"Yeah." Her eyes followed the movements of his hands, scarred, and callused from his hours in the forge, as they delicately placed the chocolate on top of the marshmallows. Then he pressed the top cracker down, just as he'd seen her do.

"Now you eat it," she said unnecessarily. When he just looked skeptically at the s'more, she sighed. "Harley…"

It looked positively tiny in his large hands, but he managed to pick it up without breaking either of the crackers. He didn't even get any marshmallow on him when he bit into it.

He chewed thoughtfully and then popped the rest of it into his mouth. She wordlessly handed him the milk. He drained it in two swallows and handed the glass back. She rinsed it out in the sink and then looked at him expectantly. "Well?"

"If we had more time, I'd make another."

"We have more time." she looked at the supplies, still out on the counter. The stove was off, but that was easily taken care of.

"No, we don't." He placed his hands on her waist and effortlessly lifted until she was sitting on the counter, her legs pushed apart by his waist. "We have other things to do." He captured her mouth, pushing his tongue deep into her mouth for a minute before pulling back. "Don't we?"

She closed her eyes and gave up the fight, knowing it was useless. "Don't you ever stop pushing?" she whispered, barely keeping a groan back as he flicked his tongue against her neck.

"Never," he breathed, pulling her hips closer to the edge and rubbing against her. "Not when there's something I want."

She tried to blink the fog of desire out of her eyes, but it stayed. Desperately, she said, "I want you to leave me alone."

"Liar." He stepped away and waited.

She sighed and slid off the counter. "I wasn't going to do this, you know. But you're just too pretty to resist."

He tugged her forward and linked her fingers with his. "Come on. It's time for bed, Abbie."

Climbing up the stairs, he asked, "Pretty?"

CHAPTER 18

Her nervousness mounted as they entered the room, and she realized what was going to happen. Then the nervousness turned into full-fledged apprehension. His jeans were already unsnapped when he closed the door to the bedroom and turned, leaning against it. "You're scared."

"Yes," she answered, her voice quivering. "Anyone would be." She twisted her fingers together and tried to look anywhere but at the bed. He walked toward her, stopping only when his chest brushed against her robe. "I'll be gentle," he promised, as he untied the belt at her waist and pushed the robe off her shoulders, letting it fall to the floor.

His fingers trailed down the front of her pajamas, releasing each button along the way until they hung open. "Take off the bottoms," he directed. She stiffened, not sure if she could. He waited a minute, then slid his hands down and tucked his fingers into the waist. Slowly, he pushed them down until gravity took over and they dropped, puddling at her feet.

"Beautiful," he murmured, his accent thickening slightly. His hands came up and pushed the sides of her top open. "Absolutely beautiful."

He leaned in and inhaled her scent, the motion a reminder that he wasn't human.

"You smell divine." He leaned closer and licked her collarbone.

"Oh..." Her head fell back on her shoulders as the desire roared back. His head moved lower, licking, and biting at her skin, drifting to her breast, then lower to her nipple. Gently, he lapped at the little point of nerves, finally taking it into his mouth and suckling.

She trembled, the sensation too much. She thrust her finger into his hair, holding him there even as she said, "I don't think I can stand anymore."

He lifted his head and his eyes had switched, gone to Were. "Then don't." He returned to her breast, switching over to the other one and giving it the same attention. His arms closed around her waist, rubbing, and massaging until she felt as pliant as a wet noodle.

"I want you on the bed."

She blinked, confused as her brain tried to muddle through the something that was said. "I'm sorry?"

His wild eyes switched to the bed. "There. Now."

His voice was so low and guttural that she couldn't understand him. But the push he gave her was unmistakable. Slowly, she went to the bed, lying down on her back as she watched him.

He nearly ripped his jeans away, shoving them off his body with a snarl, the movement so violent she was afraid he'd hurt himself. As soon as he was nude, he came for her, each step a predatory movement.

He crawled onto the bed and leaned over her, his eyes tracing her body. "I want to taste."

Her hands gripped the comforter desperately. "Harley?"

"Hush." Slowly, he lowered his body to the bed and grasped her by the thigh, pulling gently until she parted her legs. His fingers traced the bruises there for a moment, then he leaned down and licked the dark marks on her skin. She closed her eyes as his tongue wove its way up her thigh, tracing patterns only he could see. Oh God!

Deep inside, low in her stomach, her muscles clenched spasmodically, desperately trying to grasp something, anything. "Harley," she begged. He laughed, the sound low and deep. "How does it feel, Abbie?"

"It hurts," she breathed, even though that made little sense to her.

"Where? Here?" His hand slid up and rested right above her clit, rubbing gently through the crisp curls on the point of her pelvis.

Her body arched. "Oh..."

He smiled and let his hand lower to her pussy. "How about here, my beauty? Does it hurt here?" He ran a finger into her folds, spilling her syrupy juices all over until her whole cunt glistened with need.

"Yes! "

He leaned up, letting his fingers slip away from her. "I'm going to kiss you now, love."

She mewled, her hips thrusting toward him. He laughed again even as he crushed her mouth beneath his.

Her hands wandered over his chest, unable to be still. She brushed her fingertips over his nipples, and at his indrawn breath, did it again. His mouth suddenly grew more aggressive as a low, vibrating rumble rose from his chest. His hand dragged hers down his chest, across his stomach, lower, and finally wrapped her fingers around his cock.

She held him and went perfectly still. His hips thrust against her hand, and getting the idea, she slid her fingers up and down his length, happy with the feeling of so much hard, silky flesh.

"Like that?" she whispered.

He grunted and nodded briskly, his eyes closing as she made her hand go faster, up, and down. He jerked against her, groaning, and pulled away, breathing heavily.

"Enough."

She raised herself on her elbow as he moved away. "You're done?"

He pressed her shoulders back down to the bed. "Lie down, love."

She watched as he slid down her body, pressing kisses along the way to her shoulders, her breasts, and then her belly. Nervousness again coursed through her as he slid his torso between her legs, pulling them over his shoulders. "Uh, Harley, are you sure—"

His tongue darted out, passing over her clit repeatedly. She fell back with a moan, her back arching off the bed. He was definitely sure. He lapped at her, sucking, licking, and occasionally even biting at her pussy. Sometimes quick, sometimes so slow she was ready to scream.

"Do you want more?" he asked, biting the inside of her hip with just the right amount of force. He licked the area after, washing any twinges of pain away with his tongue.

"I want more," she breathed.

He thrust inside her. Deeper than a tongue should have been able to go, and she went crazy. Her body arched. She couldn't seem to keep still.

"Cum," he ordered hoarsely, letting his tongue dive deep into her again. "I want your juices on my tongue, down my throat. Cum, Abbie."

She gave a little scream when his tongue dipped into her pussy, again and again, and couldn't hold back the small explosion that released deep in her womb. He watched her through it, his tongue fucking her gently through the convulsions. When she was done, he only said, "Again," and continued. She tried to hold back each orgasm, knowing it wasn't right that she benefited from his ministrations alone, but he dragged them from her. Through each one, her body shuddered more, breaking out in a light sheen of sweat as she tried to recover enough to take control. But it didn't happen. She was so out of it that she didn't even notice when he pushed himself to his hands and knees, staring up the line of her body like she was his last meal. He gave her pussy one more lick and crawled back up her body, his cock swinging heavily with need. She lay there, panting and trying to figure out when her body had stopped obeying her.

"I'm going to fuck you." His eyes dared her to refuse him. She let her head loll, and her eyes closed. "Harley..." she panted. It was the only thing she could manage to say.

He positioned the head of his cock at her entrance, rubbing it against her slightly to get more of her moisture. "Wrap your legs around my waist, love."

She did as he ordered and held her breath as the first inch of him slid inside her. It was tight and pinched a lot more as he pushed forward. He clenched his jaw and pulled out slightly, his eyes rolling to meet hers. Then, in a forceful push, he slid fully inside.

Her back arched as she screamed from the invasion. All the breath suddenly was pushed from her body as a wave of pain washed every bit of the pleasure he'd given away.

He halted with his cock buried deep inside her. His eyes were far gone, so much the animal she had a hard time seeing the man inside. "You haven't done this before," he bit out, breathing heavily.

"No," she whispered, breathing hard as he moved inside her. He closed his eyes and surged into her again, smoothly, and there was less pain. She gave a little yelp of surprise but didn't object.

"Good?"

She nodded and closed her eyes, absorbing the feeling of him inside her, so large and deep, hitting nerves and caressing muscles that had never been touched before. His rhythm began as a simple one-two motion, but after a few minutes, it changed. It turned into something she couldn't figure out, but it was good really good. His hips pumped forward faster, harder. Sweat gleamed on his brow as he clasped her hips and tilted her pelvis higher, getting deeper penetration. It felt as if he were inside so deep he could touch her heart. He could steal it if he were so inclined. Take it away and never give it back. She wasn't even sure she cared.

The tension built deep inside, stronger than before. Panicked, she opened her eyes to see claws clutching her tightly, the nails rasping against her skin. Sharp teeth glittered in the dark, no longer human as he flung his head back and howled into the night, the sound so loud she screamed as the tidal wave took her, too. It seemed like it took forever, but it still wasn't long enough. He shuddered over her for a minute, his head back and his mouth open. Through a cloud of satisfaction, she saw his claws slip back and his teeth recede, leaving only his human face and hands. He pulled out slowly, and immediately she felt a little river of liquid leave her body. Embarrassed, she turned on her side and clasped her legs together. "I need to get up."

He stared down at her. "You didn't tell me this was your first time."

She rolled off the bed and hobbled to the bathroom as quickly as possible. She closed the door firmly behind her.

She cleaned up as quickly as she could, blushing furiously at the seed and blood she found on the insides of her legs. What a mess. No one ever spoke of how messy sex was. Certainly not in any of the outdated magazines the institute. All that had ever been in those were articles about achieving orgasm. And that definitely wasn't a problem. At least not with him.

When she came out again, he was lying on his stomach at the foot of the bed, obviously waiting for her. "Why didn't you tell me?" he asked. She rummaged around on the floor until she found her pajamas. She pulled them on, her fingers shaking slightly as she buttoned the top.

"Abbie," he said warningly.

"I thought you knew," she answered finally.

"How is that possible?"

She paused in her buttoning to glare at him. "I wasn't allowed to date in school, and I was committed just after I turned nineteen. There wasn't time for me to fool around on the side. And I really wasn't in the mood at the hospital."

He watched as she finished up the rest of the buttons. "I've never been with a virgin before."

"Congratulations. Now you have." She finished up and slid onto the bed. He was lying on the covers, so she didn't try pulling them up. He turned his body toward her, curling around her feet like some giant cat as she lay stiffly. "Did I hurt you terribly?"

She tried to glare at the ceiling, but she just couldn't do it. Her body still hummed with afterglow, and she simply felt too good to glare at anything. And then her mother's accusations entered her mind, repeating over and over again.

Slut. Whore. Tramp. With little effort, she managed to glare. "No."

His hand slid up her ankle, ducking into the leg of her PJs and caressing her skin.

"What's wrong?"

She stayed silent, her abdomen still twitching from the aftermath.

"Abbie?"

CHAPTER 19

She bit her lip. "I'm a slut."

He stopped his petting and leaned forward. "I beg your pardon?"

She smiled through the tears that were forming, hearing Killian's years of proper etiquette in the phrase. "I said," she repeated slightly louder, "I'm a slut, whore, tramp. Pick your phrase.

He crawled to the pillows and pulled her stiff body toward him. "I don't like those words," he said bitingly. "I've known whores, and you aren't one. Do you understand?"

"Not according to my mother," she said, deliberately trying to make her voice lighter than she felt.

"Your mother," he over-enunciated, "should shut the fuck up. Sex isn't wrong, Abbie. With two consenting adults, it's fun and good, and everything it's supposed to be. I want you to take pleasure in being with me. I want you to scream with it every time you cum. I get off from it. If you don't get wet when I lick your body, I'll stop. I won't ever touch you if you don't want it."

"How do you know?" she asked, studying him carefully. His face was filled with determination of another kind, the knowing kind people get when they've seen too much, or experienced things they shouldn't have. "About force, I mean? The way that you talk about it, well…"

"I've seen women forced." His eyes darkened slightly, but enough to warn her away from the topic. "Now, go to sleep," he bit out.

She studied his face for a minute before rolling to her side. "Good night."

He was silent, then she felt his hands on her body, tugging and pulling at her pajamas. "Get these off," he ordered, his hands getting rough enough to tear the material.

"Hey," she argued, trying to hold her top together. "Your father gave these to me. I love them."

"I want them off, next time I rip them from your body."

He tugged the bottoms off next and finally relaxed against her back, content with her nude body. She tried to pout. If he was so determined to rip pajamas, he should tear apart his own, not her very special pair. But then his hand drifted across her stomach in small circles, occasionally cupping her breast and rasping her nipples on the rounds, and she couldn't keep it up. It was nice. Comforting, but still intimate.

"You know," she said into the silence, snuggling closer to him, "I expected to feel different afterward."

"How so?"

"I don't know. Just different. But sex doesn't change you, does it? I mean, yes it's lovely and everything, but the result is I'm still me and you're still you. I guess I still had that teenage view of it as if I'm supposed to feel changed.

But I don't." She turned her head just enough so she could look into his eyes. "Did you feel different the first time?"

"I was relieved." He smiled slightly. "After jerking off so much, it was a relief to simply have someone to help me with the whole mess."

"Busy in your teen years, were you?" With his body and his sex drive, she didn't doubt it.

"You have no idea."

Later, when she was on the verge of sleep, she muttered, "Well, I guess old age is good for something because you definitely knew what you were doing."

He shifted against her back and leaned over her shoulder. His teeth were white against the dark as he smiled. "Go to bed."

She smirked as she fell asleep.

CHAPTER 20

She headed downstairs in mid-morning after waking up late. She took extra-long in the shower, letting the water work out the kinks and soreness from her body. It was shocking to go to bed a virgin and wake up...not. Like going to bed a brunette and waking up a blonde, although the process of losing one's virginity was a whole lot more enjoyable than getting a good dye job.

"What are your plans today?" Killian asked as she came into the kitchen. He lowered the newspaper an inch and stared at her over the top.

"I don't know. Maybe clean the barn." Rather than pull down the cereal right away, she climbed onto a stool and leaned against the counter. The reach for the cereal scared her a little bit. Her legs weren't quite feeling right after her night of sin.

"I could use your help with something." He raised his brows. "Would you mind?"

"Of course not. What do you need?"

He smiled pleasantly. "It can wait until you've finished breakfast. Now, what would you like this morning?"

An hour later, she stood in the studio and stared at Killian, hoping she hadn't heard him correctly. "You want what?"

He walked around the room, pulling out a large canvas and propping it on the easel, arranging paints, and moving lights so they fell just right. "I can hardly paint you in that," he said, pointing to her Hurtin' for a Squirtin' T-shirt. Very appropriate, considering her activities of the night before. "Don't be such a prude. Strip."

She shook her head vehemently. "I'm sorry, no. I'm not the nude type. Are you insane?"

He sighed like a martyr and glared up at the ceiling as if to ask Why me? "Wait here. I'll be right back." He loped out of the room, muttering under his breath. Seeing no other choice, she waited and was right where he'd left her when he returned carrying an elegant white dress shirt. He handed it to her and turned his back.

"Put that on, please."

She held the shirt like it was a used tissue. "I don't think this—"

"Abbie," he begged, "I'm an artist, it's what I do. It's either the shirt or nudity. Either way, I'm painting you."

Feeling particularly sacrificial, she shed her clothes, trying to give herself a little pep talk. After all, he was an artist. And they were known to be peevish and egocentric about their work.

"Okay," she announced once she had the buttons done up. "You can turn around."

He stood back and studied her, his hand tapping against his chin lightly. The shirt was one of Harley's, and on her, it hit her just above the knee. "Unbutton the top three buttons, lass."

She glanced down at the buttons, and with shaking hands unbuttoned the top three, revealing the slight swelling of her breasts and the start of cleavage. "Okay?"

"Now," He dragged the brown chair to the light and positioned it, leaving it slightly skewed. "Sit here and get comfortable because this is going to take days and days."

At first, she slumped into the chair, with her legs held tightly together and her hands anchoring the shirt down.

"Abbie..."

In the end, she curled her legs behind her and laid her head on her arms, which rested on the thick arm of the chair. It was a large chair, and she fit in it easily all curled up and content. Killian pushed her hair, so it fell in a long sheet, then stood back, a slow smile growing on his face. "I think this is perfect for you."

Satisfied, he retrieved his sketchbook and started on the preliminary sketches. "So, tell me how you feel," he ordered, as his hand moved furiously across the page. She wriggled a little. "Comfy. I'll be fine."

They let the silence reign for the next hour as he transferred the image he wanted to the sketchpad. She was content with the silence and actually closed her eyes and napped lightly for part of the time.

After an hour, he insisted she get up and stretch. When she was ready to continue, he carefully resettled her in the chair, making sure her arms were just so, and then went to the canvas and started to delicately add guidelines. "Tell me about your father. Tell me about the night he died."

She lifted her head slightly. "Why?"

He rubbed a line gently with his thumb, smudging it, and scowled at the canvas.

"I'm interested in you, and I want to hear what happened that night."

A huge wave of melancholy swept up and took her over. It was painful looking back at that memory. The Were creature was always in her mind, threatening, but the despair of losing her father was almost too much.

"We were a lot alike, my dad and me. Best pals even." She smiled at the memory.

"Mom didn't like it. I was the daughter she'd always wanted, but it was Dad I adored. He always said I looked like my grandma; his mother. I saw a picture once. I guess we look a lot alike. Mom didn't like that either."

"Why?"

She shrugged. "Grandma didn't like my mom. Said she was a city lady and that she'd drive Dad nuts on the farm. And she was right, mom hated the farm. Why they ever married I'll never know."

He smiled sadly. "Sometimes people marry for the wrong reasons. They don't realize it at the time, but it happens. My parents were one such case. They were miserable together."

"They divorced when I was fourteen," she told him. "But do you know what? It was kind of a relief. They fought so much. I remember hearing them late at night when I was supposed to be asleep. When they finally split, I didn't say a word."

He nodded in understanding. "And that night? What happened then?"

"We were driving," she said finally. "Dad liked to take the back roads when we were going to Mom's house. We'd see deer or raccoons, you know, the usual stuff."

"It sounds nice."

She nodded. "It was. But that night, we didn't see any animals. We were talking, and the next thing we knew, a huge creature was there, sitting on the side of the road."

She shivered in memory, wanting the image to dissipate, but it stayed strong in her head, as always. "I couldn't tell what it was. But I saw the woman. He was dragging her by her leg. She was bloody and broken so you could tell she was already dead. After the truck hit the tree, he ate her in front of me."

Killian stopped drawing as he listened to her voice, soft and far away, filled with memories and sadness. "What did he look like?"

She lifted her head and blinked, wiping hurriedly at the few tears that escaped to trail down her smooth skin. "It was dark. I think his coat was reddish. I know it was a guy because…well…" She shrugged and smiled nervously.

"Because everything hangs out after we shift," he supplied, going back to the canvas.

"Yeah."

He kept his tone as soothing as he could manage. "I'm sorry you had to go through that. Most of us don't prey on people, although I admit there are a few. But with every human brought down, the risk of our discovery goes up. It's a dangerous pastime to pursue if you're Were."

"Is that what we are to you?" she asked curiously. "Prey?"

He tilted his head in thought. "Well, there is certainly that aspect." He set his pencil aside and frowned. "But I don't think it's because you're human. I think it's more in the way you react when faced with a threat. It's instinctual for prey to run when threatened. When humans do the same thing, our instinct is to chase. When we chase, we want to take something down." He raised his brows and pursed his lips. "It's how we're programmed."

"So, I shouldn't ever run from someone if they're in their Were form." She nodded smartly, trying to make light of it. Ryan had said the same thing. "Okay. Got it."

Killian pulled over the paints and began digging, only stopping after he held the tubes he wanted. "You shouldn't have to worry about it. None of us would ever hurt you, in either form, or the rest of the pack wouldn't consider approaching you without one of us at your side."

The wind howled outside, but it made the warmth and security in the house that much more relaxing and lavish. "I worry about it, sometimes."

He looked up. "About what?"

She shrugged. "About the creature I saw that night if he's going to find me and kill me. Sometimes I was even sure I saw him at night, pacing around the hospital. I know it's silly because I was on so many meds, but it's there, in the back of my head."

"You know you're safe here, Abbie. No one in this house who wouldn't die to protect you." His eyes were silvery in the pale light of the room, and suddenly so powerful and aggressive that she had to fight not to cringe.

"I know," she assured him. "And I thank you for that comfort. I don't want any of you to die, though, for me or anyone else."

He picked up a paintbrush, squirted a few dabs of color on a palette, and stood in front of the canvas. "I will endeavor to meet your demands. Now, you will have to close your mouth and let me paint. I am an artist, you know."

"Yes," she giggled, "I've heard."

When they broke for lunch, she was prepared to make a break for it.

"You stay here," he insisted, wiping his hands on his once-pristine jeans, spreading a streak of slate blue across his leg. "I'll bring something up."

"I think I should get lunch." She sidled closer to the door, her freedom in sight. Quick as a snake, he had the handle in his hand and smirked. "Stay here and relax. I'll be back in a few minutes."

She watched as her escape slowly crumbled before her eyes into a pile of ashes. When the lock clicked in place, it disappeared altogether.

"That man!" She stomped her foot and waited.

Several hours later, after a lengthy discussion on the romantic prowess and proclivities of Picasso, which she just nodded her head through, curious and appalled at the same time, he finally pulled away from the canvas, wearing more paint than the painting, but pleased. "It's going well," he decided finally. "Definitely time to stop."

She uncurled from the chair, her back screaming at her. She now knew firsthand what a chick felt like just coming from its egg, uncurling its body for the first time.

"I'm tired. This is ridiculous I haven't even done anything today." She made a little squeaking noise as she stretched her arms over her head and slid out of the chair. "Is it going well, or is that just an excuse because you're tired enough to stop too?"

"It's an excuse." He methodically swirled his brushes in the mineral spirit solution and smiled. "Harley's coming up the steps and I doubt if he'll let me keep you cooped up in here all day."

She stopped in mid-stretch and looked at him. "How do you know?"

He raised his brows and tapped his ear. "Remember?"

CHAPTER 21

The door popped open, and they both looked over to see Harley step into the room, his shirt unbuttoned down the front and flapping at the sides of his chest, his jeans work-stained and worn. He was still sweaty and flushed with heat from the coals. She looked away, embarrassed. He'd seen her last night, panting, and screaming for him, completely naked and shameless. How was she supposed to act? How did he expect her to act? She only prayed Killian didn't know. Harley nodded to Killian solemnly. "You're done?"

"For today. She refused to pose nude, so I borrowed one of your shirts. I hope you don't mind."

His green eyes stared at her, pale and expressionless. "Actually," he drawled softly, watching the blush that covered her cheeks, "it looks better on her than me."

Killian finished with his brushes and carefully laid them out for the next day. "Precisely what I thought."

She thought it was a good time to leave. Jerking her head up, she turned away and grabbed her clothes, still in a pile where she'd left them. "I need to get dressed." She scurried around Harley and headed for the door, ducking her head lower as she passed him. Her breath whooshed out in relief once she was out the door and in the hall.

"I'm making beef stew tonight, Abbie," Killian called after her. "I'll need your help if you don't mind."

She bit back the retort that almost burst out of her mouth and continued to Harley's bedroom. Their bedroom, now, although it still felt strange to say that. She dressed quickly and wore the most unrevealing clothes she had, which were her overalls. They were two seconds from being donated, but so comfortable. Over an old shirt, she thought she looked quite cute in them.

Pleased with her little outfit, she hummed a tune as she went downstairs.

After dinner, rather than hang out and listen to idle conversation, she went to the studio and ended up staring at a blank sheet of her sketch pad, not sure what she was doing. No pictures came into her head, no images that were just begging to be put down. Her hand didn't even move on its own, knowing what it wanted to draw. Instead, all she had were questions. And almost all were about Harley. Behind her, the door opened. When she looked around, he was standing in the room, his back to the now closed door, and his arms folded over his chest. He didn't look pleased.

"You disappeared on me."

She turned back to the paper, and with a sigh, closed the sketch pad. "I'm sorry. I didn't think it would matter. I wanted to go somewhere and just be quiet for a while. I didn't realize I needed your permission."

He actually snarled and it wasn't at all a nice sound. She stood up and put the sketchpad back in the cabinet. When she closed and latched the doors, he was standing just to the side, his eyes searching her face.

"You regret last night."

"I don't regret it," she said immediately. "But I don't know exactly what it is you want from me. I don't understand this...thing, you have for me at all."

"I want you. That should be enough." He moved closer, crowding her against the cabinet.

It should be enough, but it wasn't. "For how long? Do I get any say in this? And what about female Weres?" she went on determinedly, giving voice to the thoughts that had been circling through her brain. "Don't they exist? Isn't there someone in your pack who has first dibs on you?"

"There are females."

She waited for him to continue, and when he didn't, she asked, "Then why aren't you with one of them? You're thirty-three. You should have kids and a wife. Why in the world are you messing around with me?"

"So, it has come to this." He sighed and moved away, his back arching for a minute. He sat down in the battered leather chair and stared at her; his eyes narrowed. Finally, he said, "You won't like it."

She slid her hands in her front pockets and shrugged. "You said you wanted me when you saw me in the hospital. I was a mess there, Harley. You can't claim to have suddenly been overcome with rapture because that doesn't fly. And if you decided I would be an easy catch, well, I can't disagree with you there. But you could have picked someone a whole lot more healthy, a lot more stable. There's something you're not saying, and I don't like it. I want to know."

"I didn't want anyone else. I wanted you."

"Right." She rolled her eyes. "And you figured this out after taking one look at my unconscious body. I may be insane, but that doesn't make me completely gullible."

A low growl came from his throat, and even as she watched, his eyes altered, changed, and reshaped to that of his other form. "I don't like it when you say that, and there is no other woman for me. Only you."

"Only me," she repeated softly, shaking her head and folding her arms over her chest. "Harley, what are you saying?"

"Come. Sit with me." He crooked his finger at her and pointed to his lap. "Sit."

She let out her breath and inched forward. His eyes were the only things that had changed, but it still made her nervous. His eyes alone were almost as scary as seeing the full package of the Were the night her father died.

She stood over him, biting her lip and avoiding looking into his eyes. "Um, what am I supposed to do here?"

"Sit and we'll talk for a while."

"Just sit," she mumbled, climbing into his lap clumsily and settling against him. It felt strange... awkward. The feeling of intimacy they'd developed the night before was completely gone. At least for her. He didn't seem to have any problems as he pulled her higher against his chest and played with the end of her braid.

"You were going to answer some of my questions," she reminded him, laying her head on his shoulder.

"Which would you have first?"

"Why aren't you married?"

"I am."

"You are," she repeated, abruptly straightening and pushing away from him. She stopped immediately when a warning growl came from his throat. "I'm leaving."

"Don't you ever say that to me."

She didn't even dare to blink or take her eyes off him. "Harley," she said carefully, her voice completely even. "Let me go."

He bared his teeth in a vicious grin. "I'm Were, Abbie. We, like wolves, mate for life. That's why I took you. That's why I have no woman from my pack. That's what you are to me. Mate."

She let out her breath and dropped her eyes to his chest, which was moving up and down as slowly as before as if there hadn't just been a tense moment. *Mate.* It echoed in her head, over and over again.

"Look at me," he ordered.

She did, but she didn't want to.

"You are my mate."

She wanted to laugh. Long and loud. Lord, what a joke. "And they thought I was insane," she quipped softly, shaking her head. "I wonder what they'd think now if I told my shrink any of this? He'd probably shove a needle in my arm and lock me in one of the safety rooms."

"Don't say that to me," he hissed. "And don't tell me what I know. You are for me. In the eyes of my people, already you are my wife."

"And that's it?" she suddenly railed. "What, you just declare it, and the whole thing is over? Don't I get a say in this?"

His mouth widened in a cynical smile. "You made your choice. Last night when I took you. If you didn't want me, then you should have said so then."

"Which is why you didn't say anything to me before. Jesus!" She hopped off his lap, half expecting him to stop her. "This is crazy. I can't believe it." She walked in a brisk circle around his chair, thinking, plotting, figuring it all out. All of a sudden, she stopped in front of him again. "Harley, this is bad."

"From where I'm sitting," he said softly, "this is incredibly good."

"No, this is bad. Very bad. To just arbitrarily be partnered with someone you hardly know?" She frowned down at him, shaking her head. "That's awful. Terrible. Fate's twisted little joke. No commitment, no affection, no great feeling. That is the very definition of bad."

His eyes rolled up and his expression darkened. "I never said there was no affection or great feeling."

She went back to walking around his chair, tapping her chin as she thought everything through. "Hmmm? Forget that. How do you know? I mean about the mate business. I'm assuming there's something, but what is it? What was it about me that you decided meant I was your mate?"

He leaned up, still staring at her. "Your scent, love."

"Right." She jerked her head in a sharp nod and then shook it. "You've got to be kidding me." Oh, this was awful! She'd been picked out of the hospital because of the way she smelled. Did life get worse than this?

"And there's no chance there's another mate out there for you? Or maybe there'll be someone else who smells the right way?"

"No."

"No? Just like that? Okay, how about this?" She nervously pushed a few loose strands of hair behind her ear and exhaled. "You and I are going to put some distance between us. No more sleeping together, no more intimacy. And we're going to go out and see if we can't find someone else who smells right."

His head moved slowly, back, and forth. "Come here. I have something else I want to tell you"

She went to him and knelt beside his chair. "Harley, I'm not trying to be mean, here. I do not doubt that for you and yours, declaring someone your mate is a very important thing and all that, but I don't think you've got the right person. I'm flattered and everything, but—

He grabbed her and jerked her onto his lap, his easy expression suddenly gone, replaced with something far more feral and harsh. "I don't fuck around. Not about anything, and I certainly wouldn't with you. You, " he snarled, "are my mate. My only. And I didn't make a mistake, Abbie. Not about this! "

She swallowed painfully and shook her head. "Harley—"

His mouth came down on hers, not hard, not painful, but soft, gentle. She opened hers and welcomed him because no matter how much she liked to argue with him, the sexual response was there whether she wanted to admit it or not.

"Please," she whispered, her tongue sliding over his, stroking it, massaging it for more pressure. All those feelings of confusion and worry joined and boiled down into old-fashioned lust. "Harley, please! "

He pulled up slowly, his eyes looking into hers. "I do love you. You may not want to hear it but don't think that this is nothing but a physical attraction. I do love you."

She laid her head against his chest and gave up the fight. "I believe you."

He settled back in the chair again, his arms around her.

He didn't make love to her that night, which she thought was a little strange, but it felt right. Her emotions were too raw, her insecurities too fresh to handle that intensity. Instead, he held her all night, keeping her at his side or spooned in front of his chest. Warmth didn't even begin to describe the amount of heat that came off this man's skin.

She woke up wrapped around him, one hand on his nape, and the other on his hip, and God, was it comfortable.

"You're awake," he said, his voice sleep roughened.

She blinked and stared at his chest, which was less than an inch from her face. Ahhh. Perfection in the morning. Was there a better way to wake up?

CHAPTER 22

Slowly, she rolled away, stretching, a soft squeak escaping from her throat as she did so. He smiled and pulled her back to him. "I was hoping you'd help me with a problem."

"Oh. Sure. What's up?"

He pulled the covers back, revealing his cock, hard and throbbing. "I am." His eyebrows rose in question. "You can tell me no. I won't like it, but I'll abide by it."

She looked at his glorious body, bare to her eyes, and couldn't quite manage to bring herself to say it. The word wouldn't seem to form in her throat. Her eyes traveled up his body and stayed on his face. She felt the desire in her body, pooling quickly in her loins, already dangerously close to the breaking point.

"Yes. " She lunged for him, her hands itching to touch him, her lips seeking the pressure of his. "Harley…"

"I know babe." He pulled her mouth to him and latched onto her, sucking, and swiping his tongue inside, his hand already on her breast and teasing, stroking her nipple. It stiffened immediately.

She wiggled with impatience across his chest, her hands exploring his body, chest, sides, and hips. He was so wonderful to touch that she'd never get enough. And because there was so much of him, she doubted that would be a problem.

"What do you want?" he whispered against her mouth. "What can I give you?"

She stopped her hand's caress over his thigh, confused over his question. "What do you mean?"

He pushed her hair over her shoulder and kissed her forehead. "I mean, how do you want it? What are your fantasies? What have you dreamed of?"

"You know where I was. In that place, I didn't dream. I had nightmares, and that's it. As far as this type of thing goes," she shook her head, "I'm a blank slate. I just want."

"You want," he repeated, his hand returning to her nipple and gently squeezing. She sucked in a breath and closed her eyes. "I want you," he whispered. "One day, in the change, but I'll settle for skin for now."

She barely heard him. His mouth immediately latched onto her other nipple, and his mouth pulled at the flesh, rhythmically using pressure to make her squirm. She slid her hands into his hair and held him there, thrusting her chest out, hoping he'd take the hint and keep going.

He did.

"The other," she breathed. "Harley, please…"

He let her nipple slide from his mouth, and when he did, she saw his eyes changed as before. "Have your breasts always been this sensitive?"

"Jesus, you expect me to think now? "

A rough laugh escaped his throat even as he took her neglected nipple into his mouth and gently caressed the other, plucking it delicately between two fingers. She cried out from the barrage of sensations.

She was content for a while, but soon her whole body was on fire. It flooded her veins, traveled into her skin, but most especially down to her pussy. She dripped with need any other time would have been embarrassing. But with him at her breast, and his lovely body before her, she didn't have room for embarrassment and gave herself up to the desire.

He pressed on her lower back until she could feel his cock, swollen and hard against her stomach. She moved, sliding against him gently, and his mouth opened wide, releasing her nipple as his head went back and his eyes closed.

"Christ."

She took his mouth with her own, thrusting her tongue delicately at him. His hand fisted in her hair, anchoring her head while his other hand kept pressure on her back.

He growled and thrust his hips against her. She moaned and ground her mouth against his, needing more. The feel of dampness against her stomach keyed her into the fact that he was just as needy as she was.

"I know," he whispered roughly. He kissed her, and then abruptly rolled them over so that he was on top. "Are you ready?"

Ready for what? The heat in his eyes said it was something different, but what exactly he had planned, she didn't know. But then, she didn't care, either. He got up on all fours and crooked his finger at her. "Come here, beauty. We're going to try something new right now."

She stayed where she was for a second, stretched on the bed, her legs separated and her breath coming in little pants. He wanted her to get up now?

He smiled tightly, but helped pull her to her knees, and then pushed her down so that she was in front of him, on her hands and knees.

She looked at him over her shoulder, even as he pressed down on her spine, which caused her butt to dip up. Very embarrassing, she thought, but he seemed to be in rapture.

"Beautiful," he murmured, his hand sliding down her spine. "Spread your legs, love."

She let out a shuddering breath to hell with embarrassment. The way he stared at her; she was the equivalent of a meal in front of a starving man.

"I'm going to take you like this now. But, one day, I'll have you like this in the change."

She opened her mouth to refute his declaration, but nothing came out except a moan as he delicately slid his fingers through her folds, rubbing against her clit just barely, but enough to make her want to scream.

"Would you stop teasing me?" She glared at him over her shoulder. His finger entered her fully, pushing in and sliding out. He pushed two fingers in, and her eyes rolled back.

"I think you're ready," he said, pulling his fingers out and sucking them clean. He grasped his cock and rose on his knees, already pressing the head at her opening.

"Abbie?" he growled.

"Please," she begged, rocking backward, the feel of him as smooth as silk. He surged forward, burying his cock deep inside her. "Good?"

"Mmm." She closed her eyes and hummed as the feeling of him entering her, again and again, took over her body. For her, there was nothing else except him, the curve of her back, the feel of his chest lying against her, and his cock, constantly moving, burrowing inside her. It was like nothing else. Certainly, nothing she'd ever felt before.

His hand came around her body and fondled her breast, squeezing and plumping, until everything was too much, and she cried out her body tightening around him.

"Do you doubt me, mate?" he taunted, his lips so close they brushed the shell of her ear. "Do you doubt I'd know my match, my woman when I saw her?"

All the air whooshed out of her lungs. She didn't care what he said, his cock was huge, and hard enough that she could feel every little bump and ridge as it plundered her body. So hard, the taut skin so velvety, he kept moving rhythmically inside her, over and over, slowing getting stronger and rougher with each thrust of his hips, until at the end, she was damp from head to toe with sweat, and his chest slid lightly against her back and absolutely every cell in her body was tied up and twisted in a painful knot, just waiting to be released. And then he stopped. He panted against her back and bit down gently on her shoulder. She shivered and tried to thrust her hips back, except this time he didn't allow it.

"Uh-ah. Not yet."

She squeezed her eyes closed and tried to concentrate on the rioting, pulsing lust deep inside her. Everything throbbed. Everything felt swollen to about twice its size. No doubt she'd orgasm if he so much as let her legs move. His right hand slid down her arm and covered hers where it supported her weight on the bed. "This. Between us. It's proof we're mated." His free hand rubbed her nipple, plucking at it with just enough pressure. "I love how it feels when I'm inside you. So tight, so hot. You squeeze my cock like nothing else, Abbie."

"Oh God." She tilted her head back and canted her hips forward the tiny millimeter he allowed. "Just—just finish, Harley. Please, finish."

She screamed as he suddenly pounded inside her, and her body went up in flames. The rippling started immediately and went on even after he stiffened and came inside her.

They crumpled to the bed together, both too satisfied to speak. She smiled in satisfaction and finally broke the silence. "If I'd known you'd have this effect on me, I think I would have climbed into your bed the first night I was here."

He pulled her against him and curled his body around her back, his chest rumbling.

"I wouldn't have turned you away."

She smiled.

She woke up finally around noon and spent the day in the studio with Killian, who insisted they get some of the portrait done. She argued, pouted, bitched, and cried, and she still ended up half-naked and posed in the chair as he painted.

They broke just before five, with him wanting to get dinner on. She dressed, and then went down to the kitchen, picking at the specks of paint he had accidentally splashed over her arms.

The boys were already in the kitchen. Killian had a bottle of wine open and a glass half-filled with the dark red liquid at his elbow. Ryan toasted her lightly with his glass as she came in. Harley stared at her and quietly sipped, somehow making the act of drinking seem obscenely graceful.

"Good evening." She ducked her head and scooted into the room.

"Glad you could join us." Ryan tipped his glass up and emptied it.

"Would you like some?" Killian asked, chopping onions at a furious rate.

"No. Thanks. What do you want me to do?" For a second, she was dizzied by his speed. It was impossible that his hands were moving that fast. She watched, entranced as he pulled a large onion forward, halved and quartered it, and then went to work. Ten seconds later, it was cut into fine, perfect little pieces, and he was already working on another. His eyes were still glossy with tears which made her feel a little better. At least being a werewolf didn't mean you weren't affected by onions like everyone else.

"Ryan has declared that he needs a steak, and since I have some perfect ones, just delivered yesterday I bowed to his lesser judgment. But," he held up his knife "you can wash the potatoes if you don't mind."

She busied herself first with the potatoes, then went out and set the table, her mind on other things as she placed the plates and silverware. Foremost in her mind was Harley, because lately, she couldn't get him out of her mind. What in the world she going to do with him? Sure, history was filled with women being stuck with men they didn't want, but if she was honest, she had to admit that she wanted him. She wasn't necessarily in love with him, but there was a definite pull in her heart, growing stronger every hour he was around. Especially when he was all dark and brooding, which was how he was now. Ryan and Killian were speaking easily, she kept expecting him to cut in sometimes, but he didn't. He kept up the silent glowering, most likely directed at her. She could practically feel the weight of his eyes on her back, which was weird. And what exactly did he have to be pissy about? He'd gotten everything he wanted. She was in his bed, they'd had great sex, and now it was dinner time. Steaks, no less. He should be ecstatic. She surveyed the table critically, and after she was sure everything was there, returned to the kitchen and leaned against the doorway, watching as Killian removed a huge package of steaks from the refrigerator.

"Now," he said, looking at each of them in turn, "Harley, you'll eat four, Ryan you'll probably have the same. I'll have three and Abbie…" He turned to her and held up a huge piece of beef. "One?"

Her brow crinkled as she stared at the meat. "Jesus. What are those? Like twenty-five ounces? Yeah. One will do it."

"Don't worry," he said, throwing the steaks into a pan and heading for the door to the porch. "Someone will finish it." He popped open the door and entered the cold, not even bothering to get a jacket.

"He's grilling?" She turned to Ryan and pretended not to see the way Harley's eyes were narrowing. "Grilling in below-zero temperatures? Is he insane?"

"What can I say, the man likes his steaks, and he doesn't fuck around when cooking them." Ryan shrugged his shoulders.

"Apparently."

Killian came back in, bringing a rush of cold air with him pan absent of raw steak but streaked with watery blood. He hummed softly as he went over and rinsed the plate off, and she got an idea.

"Do you use gas or charcoal?"

He almost sneered in his oh-so-proper accent, "Lass, anyone who cooks knows that gas is a poor substitute for charcoal. I'm appalled you suggested that I would even think to skimp when it comes to something as important as cooking steaks."

"Sorry, I was just asking." She waited until he was occupied again before calmly bending down and digging through the cupboard. The marshmallows were in the front, right where she'd left them.

"What are you doing?" Killian's brow furrowed as he eyed the bag of marshmallows with suspicion. "You aren't going to make those awful cracker things, are you?"

She looked up from the cabinet, a pack of chocolate bars in hand. "Yeah. So?"

He shuddered delicately. "They're so messy."

She stared at his paint-covered pants but politely remained silent. "But they're good."

CHAPTER 23

"You can make one for me," Ryan offered, leaning on his elbow against the counter. "I haven't had one of those things in years."

"You can make your own." She set the Grahams alongside her other supplies and stood up; her work done.

After the steaks and potatoes were finished, she and Killian set the food on the table while Ryan filled glasses.

"Wine?" he asked Harley, who had followed him into the room.

"Please."

"For me, as well," Kilian said, coming through the door with a basket of baked potatoes.

With his eyes sparkling, Ryan turned to Abbie, his eyebrows raised. "Okay, let me guess. Grape juice?"

"You are such an ass." She shook her head at him and rolled her eyes, turning back toward the kitchen. Grape juice indeed. "I will have you know," she told him over her shoulder, "that I will progress to harder substances when I feel ready. After years of God only knows how many sedatives, it's probably a good idea that I take it slow, don't you think?"

His laughter stopped and he tilted his head. "Oh. Actually, that makes a lot of sense."

"You're still an ass." Just before she made it to the doorway, she was pulled to a halt. Strong arms wrapped securely around her and pulled her to the side. Harley's arms hooked around her waist and held her completely still.

"What are you doing?" she whispered, struggling against him. Even as she tried to get away, she saw Ryan smile and shake his head, passing them as he went to the refrigerator. "They don't need to know absolutely every detail; I'd like to keep some things private."

"I don't like being ignored." His head lowered to the curve of her neck, and he inhaled deeply. "You smell good."

A blush crept up her neck and face. She wanted to groan when Killian smiled over at them as he took his seat at the head of the table.

"It's called soap. Marvelous invention. Harley, stop."

"Why?" He shifted her closer and kissed her neck softly.

"Because!" She pulled her head back, glaring at him. "They'll think that we're…"

She widened her eyes to get her point across.

"They know we're mated, Abbie." His eyes were steady and pale, tilted exotically at the corners. He was lovely even when he was being a pain.

"It's not like it's a secret," Ryan added, coming out of the kitchen with the milk. "We're not human. I can smell him on you." He held the jug up for her perusal.

"Any complaints with this?" He went over to the table, whistling as he filled her glass. She groaned and wished the floor would open up and swallow her on the spot, but it stayed stubbornly firm beneath her feet. "That's not what I needed to hear."

"Kiss me," he ordered, pulling her chest flush with his. "And I'll let you go." He didn't give her any time to maneuver away, and lowered his mouth to hers, making his lips soft and sensual.

Almost helplessly, she responded to him, forgetting about her embarrassment as she slid her arms over his neck and held on for all she was worth. He pulled away and nuzzled below her ear. "Now you can go." He released her and took his seat at the table.

Ryan smiled coyly as she sat in her chair still in a daze. She didn't comment as the food was passed around, not even when someone dumped a huge steak on her plate.

Halfway through the meal, the doorbell rang. Killian wiped his mouth and set his napkin beside his plate as he got up. "I'm sure that's Cormac. He wanted to speak with you tonight, Harley."

She heard the door open, and then low voices talking. Killian came to the table with a younger man, around Ryan's age, following close behind. He was shorter than both Ryan and Harley, and thinly built, but with the promise of greater mass as he aged. His features were plain but pleasant, his hair a dirty blonde in the light of the dining room. The minute he saw Harley he nodded respectfully, his eyes downcast. "Harley."

Harley stood up and gave him his hand. There was no shaking, but their hands clasped together for a moment before Harley released him and motioned him toward a chair. "Join us."

Cormac sat across from Ryan while Killian went to get an extra setting.

"Here." Ryan forked over one of his steaks once Cormac had a plate. "You can have this one since Abs will give me most of hers anyway."

Cormac looked over and smiled at her, nodding his head just slightly. "It's a pleasure."

"What do you have?" Harley asked.

Cormac braced himself. "Jaxon is speaking to pack members, spreading rumors about a challenge you refused."

It was like a wave of arctic wind suddenly blew into the room. The men were so still, she wasn't even sure if they were breathing. And once again, she was in the middle of a conversation about challenges, except this time she had a better idea of what they were talking about. And Jaxon, that name kept popping up, too, and every time it seemed to be worse and worse. She wasn't sure what a challenge was, but it didn't sound good.

"Really?" Harley murmured, laying his fork and knife aside and sitting back in his chair.

"Yes. Most don't believe it, knowing you well enough, especially after your last challenge. But few would be happy to see you thrown from the pack for a refusal." He looked between Harley and Killian, and then down at his plate. Ryan whistled. "They've got to be idiots to believe that one. They'd have better luck trying to take him down themselves."

Killian inclined his head and stared at Abbie, steel in his voice as he said, "Why don't you tell us what you know about Jaxon, Abbie."

She sucked in her breath as they all turned toward her. Four sets of inhuman eyes settled on her and waited expectantly. She shook her head. "I don't know what you mean."

"What do you mean?" Harley questioned softly. His head tilted in that feral way they all had. "What do you know, Abbie?"

Her eyes flew to Killian and narrowed. He raised his brows. "She asked me about him while you were on a run. She claims to have heard the name from you and Ryan."

"I did," she argued. "You talked about him at the pub." Ryan elbowed her side. She turned and glared at him. "Knock it off."

"Why are you protecting him?" Ryan shook his head at her. "I don't get it. Just tell us what you know, and it's done. We can take care of the rest, Abbie."

"Are you going to kill him?"

Ryan looked at Harley his eyes remained stoic and still locked on her.

"Does it matter?" he asked, his tone easy and smooth.

She wanted to laugh hysterically. Of course, it mattered! "All I want to know is what he's done that's so terrible." He tried to have you kidnapped, her mind screamed, but Harley had done that himself, taking her from the hospital without a thought to what her wishes were, or that of her mother. Issac had even admitted that rape wasn't part of his order from Jaxon. That had been his choice, and he'd paid for it with his life.

"What are you looking for, Abbie?" Killian's eyes searched her face, trying to see her secrets. "What do you need to know before you'll tell us how you know about him?"

The men's attention was like a lead weight tied around her neck, dragging her down. She exhaled slowly and bowed her head, bracing herself. "If I tell you, and you kill him, it'll be my fault."

No one spoke for a moment, and the uncomfortable silence grew. She looked up, seeing the intent in each of their eyes as they stared at her. Ryan was the one who broke the silence. "Abbie, Harley will have to fight him. And," he added, his eyes so dark they were almost black, "he's going to kill him. It's only a matter of when."

A half gasp, half laugh escaped her. "That's supposed to make me feel better?"

Harley lept to his feet and leaned on the table with his hands on each side of his plate. He watched her, his eyes menacing and glittering with violence. "You will tell me."

She shrank beneath the force of his glacial anger. Inside, every little piece of bravery was shriveling on the vine of courage, dying under the ice of his demeanor. She took a deep breath and raised her eyes to him, flinching slightly, and clung to the last bit of backbone she possessed. "No."

His nose flared slightly. "No?"

"No," she repeated, her voice no more than a whisper. "I'm sorry."

His hand crashed down on the table; the heavy table jumped from the pressure. Two dishes broke leaking vegetables over the tablecloth.

"Abbie," Killian said soothingly, "we need to know how you know his name. It's important."

She shook her head. "I'm sorry, but I can't. If you'll please excuse me." She threw her napkin on the table and pushed her chair out, practically leaping away and running from the room.

They watched her go in silence. Killian turned back to his plate and sighed heavily.

"Try and find out as much as you can."

Cormac nodded and picked up his fork, finishing his steak quickly, obviously eager to be gone.

Harley went to the sidebar and poured himself a healthy shot of whiskey, downing it almost in one swallow. "I want to know how she knows his name."

"We did talk about him in the bar," Ryan said dully.

"Yes, and if she'd been curious then, she would have asked. She knows something about him, somehow." Killian tapped his chin in thought as Harley resettled himself at the table cutting his steak in controlled, vicious movements. "Cormac, see if Issac was aligning himself with anyone. Harley, we need to be sure about this if you're to call Jaxon out before the next full moon."

"I'll see what I can find," Cormac said. "But Issac was pretty solitary. It may be difficult to find anyone willing to talk about him."

"Do what you can." Killian turned to Harley; his eyes dark with memories. "You know how Nora died. If this goes how I think it will, you'll be forced to make the same choice. Remember it's better to have her angry with you, even horrified and scared, rather than dead in the hands of your enemies."

"I won't live with that bastard threatening my life and family every other month," Harley snarled. "He dies."

She was shaking too much to sleep, adrenaline was running amok in her system making her too jumpy and hyper to even hope for sleep, so she took a bath in the wonderfully large claw-foot tub. After filling it up nearly to the brim, she climbed in and reclined against the end, sitting as far down in the water as she could.

It took forty-five minutes, but eventually, her body slowed to normal speed, and she stopped feeling like her heart jumped out of her chest. She was left feeling utterly exhausted wasted away to nothing.

She got out when the water cooled, drying herself with an almost detached air. It was like her body didn't even belong to her anymore. She was apart, floating freely above everything, untouched and safe. Except it was a lie. Nothing was safe. She cried herself to sleep.

"Wake up, Abbie..."

She opened her eyes groggily and blinked into the dark. Harley leaned over and kissed her softly. Still sleep-muddled, she opened her mouth to him immediately, inviting the seduction of his tongue. As the kisses deepened, her hands ran over his stomach, loving the feel of his hard silkiness.

"I want you," he breathed against her lips, sucking lightly on her bottom lip. He licked it with his tongue, then bit down, using his teeth to wring a moan from her. Everything below her waist was suddenly wide awake and wanting him. She clutched at him, digging her fingers into the heavy muscles of his chest as the desire built. Under her hands, his muscles flexed and jumped. He stayed on all fours above her, bending down every time he sucked her skin or lapped at her nipple. He buried his hand in her hair, angling her head better, allowing his tongue deeper access. His breathing became harsh with the thrusts of his tongue in her hot mouth, growing deeper and wilder until she was sure she was going to go out of her mind if she didn't get him inside her.

"Give me more," he ordered harshly, his face savage in the shadows. She blinked slowly, trailing her fingers up, along his sides, feeling the bumps of his ribs, the hard muscles of his chest, and the slight contraction of his nipples as she attended to them. She swirled her fingers around them until he hissed and groaned. She pushed herself up on her hands and kissed the column of his throat. When he rumbled in pleasure, she gently nipped at his skin, trailing lower to his collarbone. His breath whooshed out like a steamer. "Lower," he gritted, pushing at her shoulders gently. "Please, love. Lower. "

She moved down his body, sliding her legs between his, licking and kissing his chest. She stopped at his nipples and laved the hard nubs with her tongue, over and over until his body shook with tension. His whole body was like that of a statue, hard with tension, but hot to the touch. There was nothing cold about him. He ran hot all the time. His teeth gritted. "Lower. "

Taking a deep breath, her hand captured his cock, squeezing it gently before she wiped the pre-cum off the tip. "Here?" she whispered, fondling his testicles softly with her free hand.

CHAPTER 24

He lowered his head, watching her, his eyes filled with wild things she couldn't ever hope to understand. "Do it."

She wasn't the kind of girl who did things like this. It was the last thought that had her beating the fear down and going for broke. She lay beneath him, curved up at the waist, and licked his penis, the first swipe of her tongue shy and curious. He tasted just as he was slightly salty but spicy.

"God, Abbie!" His breath hitched in his chest as she took him in her mouth, sucking on his length. Her hand crept up and wrapped around the base of him, moving in time with the pulsing of her mouth.

"Deeper," he grunted, as he thrust his hips slightly. She took it but gasped. "Relax your throat," he gritted out and flexed his hips again. She closed her eyes and let her body feel, without the visuals, and then she found she could take him deeper. And her reactions to him got stronger with just the feeling of him moving in and out of her mouth. It made it more sensual, and special. It made it easier to hear every gasp and groan that came from his throat, made it easier to feel every thrust of his hips, every bunch of his ass. She realized how much more there was to desire and sensuality than just the visual. She heard the sheets tear as she swirled her tongue beneath the head of his cock. He gasped, the sound so deep she wasn't sure what it was at first. "I'm going to cum and you're going to take it." His hand threaded into her hair and held her head to him. Her hands clenched against his thighs, and with a shout, his seed shot from him, the spurts hitting the back of her throat.

She held onto him through his release, obediently swallowing all he gave her. When he was done, she let his cock slide from her mouth, licking the head just before he pulled away. She slid back up to the pillows, not sure if she should be shocked by her behavior or brazen it out. He was on his knees before her. His head stayed bowed, and his eyes closed. "Was I too rough?"

"No," she whispered. "It was nice." She rolled to her side and curled in on herself, wondering where her pajamas were, probably on the floor. She glanced behind her to check.

"We're not done," he said, his voice almost vicious.

She shivered slightly. "I'm fine. You don't have to—"

"I want to fuck. Hard, long, all night."

She stared at him for a minute. "But, you just finished. Don't you need to wait?"

His hand reached down and grasped his cock, already hot and hard again. He sat back on his heels and masturbated for her, his movements slow and methodical. His head fell forward again as he watched her from under his brow. "I don't need long. I'm good all night, and I want to fuck you now."

He tugged her forward, lifting her onto his lap. His mouth searched for hers, found it, and plundered, seeking her tongue. His hand manipulated her higher until her heat rubbed against his cock, over and over until she was out of her head to have him.

"Do you want me?" he asked her harshly, pulling away.

She couldn't speak, every nerve in her body was too fired up for her to get a word out. In answer, she slid her hand to his nape and tugged him back down to her, needing some part of him inside her. She gasped against his mouth, demanding his attention. He groaned and kissed her, pulling her legs around his waist as he positioned her. His jaw clenched a second before he pulled her down over him, impaling her in one fast motion.

The scream died in her throat as he used his hips brutally, pulling her off before he jerked her down again. She gasped and her eyes closed as she absorbed the sensations of his aggressive manipulations. Her hips rocked against him, searching for more stimulation, rubbing closer and closer against his smooth skin with every surge of his hips.

"Do you like that?" he asked, abruptly stopping the movements. She cried out, frustrated and wanting. With a hard smile, he slid a finger over her clit, rubbing the fevered flesh delicately, once, twice, and then he stopped.

"What are you doing?" she whispered, her whole body left wanting. She needed more. Not much, just enough to release tension and she needed it now!

He stared at her, all menacing as his jaw clenched. "Who told you about Jaxon, Abbie?"

She sucked in a breath and rolled her eyes to the ceiling, trying to get herself under control. "Don't," she groaned. "Don't do this to us. Don't ruin this!"

"I want the person who told you about Jaxon," he ordered his eyes piercing orbs in the darkness of the room. He pushed his hips at her slightly, enough to make her shudder, then he stopped again. "Where did you hear that name?"

She gasped and closed her eyes, needing the peace of darkness under such a painful onslaught. "The...pub," she said through gritted teeth.

"Don't lie!"

He threw her off his lap and onto the bed. She landed with a bounce, and he came down on top of her a second later. He pulled her arms over her head and locked them with one hand. "Now," he said through gritted teeth. "Tell me."

She breathed slowly, in and out, and felt the remnants of the pre-orgasm in her body, still there, but cooling with each breath. She closed her eyes against him and turned her head, taking the only escape she could. "No."

He settled himself between her thighs and brushed his cock against her heat. "I want to know."

Slowly, she shook her head against the pillow and whispered, "I'm sorry."

"Tell me!"

"I can't," she cried, tears escaping beneath her eyelids.

"Damn you," he said darkly, and in one move, he slid inside her, moving quickly as he fucked her, his mouth clamped shut and fury in his eyes. A single tear escaped from the corner of his eye, only to be brushed away as he pressed his lips to hers, desperately seeking her tongue.

Her eyes flew open the moment his cock touched her, and he began moving with harsh, jerky thrusts. She tried to pull her hands free, but he kept them prisoner.

"Don't stop," she begged, pulling her mouth away and winding her legs around his hips to keep him inside. "Don't leave me like that again."

"Shut up," he hissed, and surged into her harder, enough to make her gasp. His free hand crept down and caressed her clit, then dipped slightly lower, massaging her gently.

It was so good. So good! Stronger than anything else, sweeter, yet more bitter. It was so hot, each buildup to her orgasms sending her higher and higher until she couldn't take it anymore. She burst suddenly, crying out with it. He removed his hand, and grasped her hips, pulling them higher over his arms as he continued thrusting through her orgasm. He grunted with each move, then shuddered over her and buried himself one last time, as deeply as he could, gritting his teeth as he came in long waves. He let his head fall to her shoulder and lay still.

The silence lay between them, uncomfortable and foreboding. He pulled away from her and settled on his side. "I want to know who told you about Jaxon."

She turned away from him, a tear running down her cheek. "I heard it in the pub."

He turned, snarling and deadly. "Stay silent, I don't give a fuck, but never, ever lie to me again. " He got up and jerked his jeans back on. The door slammed behind him as he left.

The silence surrounded her as she tried to make plans. One thing was certain... mate or no, it was time to leave.

CHAPTER 25

Harley returned to bed at three in the morning. He slipped under the covers not saying a word to her and went to sleep. Abbie waited two hours before she got up. She dressed quickly and threw a few things into a bag. She let herself out of the house without a backward glance.

She stole his keys off the hook by the front door and used them to unlock the garage. Once in, she flipped on the lights and surveyed the possibilities. Her father had taught her about seven years ago, but she wasn't good at it. She just hoped she wouldn't screw up too badly. Two cars in the garage, Harleys' Bronco and a small compact. Off to the side was Ryan's bike. Guilt tugged at her heart for taking one of their cars. Of course, she planned on parking it somewhere for one of them to pick up once she got to a bus station, but still, it wasn't a nice thing to do. Sighing, she took the compact, rationalizing that it was the least expensive, and in the case that something did go wrong, she wouldn't be paying for it for the rest of her life. *Is this a good idea?* she asked herself, sitting in the driver's seat. Her immediate answer was an emphatic *No!* But no matter how she tried, she couldn't see any other options. Harley wouldn't stop pushing, prodding, and manipulating her until he had the information he wanted, and then he'd go on a rampage and Jaxon would die, all because she couldn't keep her mouth shut. And a death on her head wasn't something with which she could live.

Taking a breath, she started the car and backed up.

Driving was easier than she expected, although after she thought about it a bit more, how difficult could it be with only two pedals? But the snowy roads gave her a bit of a problem, and the first time she hit a large drift, she drove over the fluffy white snow slowly, wincing as her tires spun. But she didn't slide and convinced herself it was a good sign. She'd be okay, and it would all work out. She'd find a nice little town and get a job at a restaurant or bookstore. She would even get her mother to send her birth certificate and social stuff, so she'd be legal. And then maybe, after she was settled and secure and a comfortable amount of time had passed, she'd go see Harley again. She shivered at the thought. *Maybe not.*

Jaxon watched as the little blue car went by at a staid speed. The small form hunched behind the wheel was easily identified making him smile.

He pulled out his cell phone, hit speed dial, and waited until it was picked up. "Get your ass up. His bitch is going to be driving past your place in five minutes."

There was silence on the other end, then the voice said, "You got it."

He slid the phone back into his pocket watching as the car disappeared slowly over the hill.

The ringing was driving him crazy. Ryan reached out for the phone blindly, desperate to make it stop. "Hello?" he mumbled.

"Ryan!" Cormac yelled. "Christ, man, get up and find Harley. We've got movement from Jaxon's end. I think they've got his mate."

Ryan lay still for a second, then the sentence registered in his brain. He shot up in bed and was out of his room and down the stairs in seconds. He barged into Harley's room, his eyes wild and searching.

"Fuck!" She wasn't there.

He threw the phone at Harley, who turned and caught it in his raised hand. "Get up you son of a bitch!" Ryan shoved his hand through his hair and glared. "Your girl's cut and run." He whirled around and ran up the stairs to get dressed. Fifteen seconds later, Harley's howl shook the entire house.

Abbie looked at her position in the road, or more accurately, in the ditch. It wasn't her fault the car slid into a bank. It was the squirrel's. She leaned back against the seat with her eyes closed and called the squirrel every inappropriate word she could think of, ending with the mother of all words, fucker. It felt good to say out loud, so she did for about twenty seconds, ending by slamming her hands against the steering wheel. The car gave no reaction.

"Need help?" someone shouted through her window.

She looked over and saw a truck stopped just five feet behind her. A bearded man who looked like Tormund Giantsbane from Game of Thrones stood beside it, his form shrouded by a heavy leather coat. He was smoking a cigar as he leaned on his truck. She opened the door and got out, she was a disgrace, a failure, not to drive more than an hour without getting stuck. Harley would probably chain her to his bed for the rest of her natural life.

"I'd appreciate it," she said, looking over at him and trying to appear competent. "I was trying to avoid hitting a squirrel."

For some reason, he laughed at her, so hard tears streamed from his eyes. He had to wipe them away with his leather gloves, twice.

"Well," he wheezed, finally standing straight, "I appreciate it. That's the best laugh I've had in about years." He reached out a hand to her. "My name's Elijah Haren, lass."

Abbie shook his hand. "Nice to meet you, I'm Abbie Marsh."

His hand closed over hers for a moment, and then she was yanked forward, her arms wrenched behind her back.

She gasped at the sudden pain of it and then shrieked as something cold was tightened around her wrists, locking them together.

"Sorry to do this to you, Abbie," he said easily. "My Alpha's called on me, and I don't like to disappoint."

She tried to run, but he kept a hold of her arms. "Harley told you to tie my wrists together?"

He snorted. "Harley, no. I got nothin' to do with that asshole. I'm talking about the true pack leader, Jaxon. He'd like to meet with you for a while." He pulled her toward his truck and tossed her in before climbing behind the wheel. The engine roared to life as he cranked the wheel, turning around in the road. "You should have stayed safe, locked away in that house of Killian's. But it's their bad luck, and good for us."

"Why?" She tried to twist her wrists free. It hurt, but less than it should have. The feeling was already leaving her fingertips. It would only be a matter of time before she wouldn't even be able to bend her fingers.

"It's going to throw the asshole off for a while, he's going to come charging to the rescue, unprepared, and try to take you back. I can't wait. I'm going to rip out his fucking spine." He chortled over the thought.

The easily said threat froze her blood in her veins and the image of Harley dead solidified in her head. "He's not going to come for me. He doesn't even like me right now." It was the truth and would only become more so after he learned she'd left him. He looked at her incredulously. "I can smell him on you, lass. That prick fucked you less than eight hours ago. No use lying 'bout it." He winked at her and turned back to the road. "Yup. It's strange to be Were, although I don't have any basis for comparison, you understand. We used to be mighty. Predators among sheep, you might say. Anything in our woods, we'd kill, didn't matter if it were little Maggie from school or a stray cow from the farm down the road. If it was walkin' on a full moon night, we took it down and damned the consequences. We always made a good meal of it.

"We had one guy," he continued, ignoring the look of horror on her face, "a real old-timer. He liked to skin them first, while they still squirmed. Only afterward would he eat them."

Her mouth fell open, and bile rose in her throat. "Stop."

He smiled over at her. "Don't ever confuse us with your humans. Other than the appearance, we're nothing alike. Our brutality is too dominant. I'll have to kill Harley, and if not me, then Jaxon, because if he's left alive, he's going to fuck us six ways to Sunday for touching you. Don't get me wrong, I don't blame him for it, that's as it should be. He's Were, and he'll react like one."

She sat stunned, her bound wrists forgotten. His words echoed in her head, so awful she couldn't get them out. But they served as a reminder she'd forgotten what they all were. She'd made a mistake. They looked and talked like humans, but they weren't. They were animals far more than humans, and she couldn't forget that.

"I want to go home," she announced, staring straight ahead.

"Sorry," he replied, sounding anything but. "We're going over to Nessa's house. Jaxon's meeting us there. Besides, she wants to see the bitch who took her out of the running for Harley's bed."

It hurt to think of another woman in Harley's bed, more than she wanted it to.

"Does she love him?" she asked softly.

He snorted. "Fuck no. She's a strong bitch. She wants the power that goes along with fucking him. Nessa was kind of pissed when she found out he had a little human to do."

"Why does Jaxon want me?"

He glanced at her, his lips twisting slightly. "It seems you have a history with him. He met you a few years back. Don't know why he didn't take you out then."

It took her a minute to put two and two together, but when she did, a whole new horror surfaced and stared at her with murderous eyes.

"Oh God."

"Yup. For you, anyway."

She stayed silent the rest of the drive, trying to come up with anything that would get her free. Elijah happily continued chattering the rest of the way, recounting the most horrible stories she'd ever heard, and laughing every time she flinched during the telling.

He pulled up at an old homestead with dilapidated barns. He got out of the truck and dragged her behind him, making her stand still as he looked at her restraints. He whistled. "Damn, you did a number on your wrists." He leaned down and jerked her hands up at the same time, which made her yelp as her shoulders were stretched in a way that was painful and not entirely possible. When she felt the wet lap of his tongue on her forearms, she tried to jerk away. He retaliated by roughly pushing her down to the ground, keeping her still with a knee in her back. "Don't move," he ordered, his voice deep and rough, all amusement gone. His tongue licked her wrists, moving below the ties in long swipes. She cringed, trying not to think about what he was doing or why he was doing it, and thankful that everything below the restraints was numb.

"What are you doing?" someone screeched from the right.

CHAPTER 26

Abbie lifted her head from the snow, gasping as she was dragged to her feet by a rough hand on her bound wrists. A woman was striding toward them, tall and pretty, with a narrow frame and sleek muscles. She had cruel eyes with hate as they stared at her.

"This here is Harley's little bitch," he said happily, absently wiping the blood from his mouth with the back of his hand. "She's sweet, too. No wonder he keeps her around."

The woman, Nessa, Abbie assumed, came forward, a sneer on her face as she studied her. "She's a runt. Christ, what's he thinking taking a little piece like this?"

"Maybe it's not just her blood that's sweet," he suggested smirking and wiggling his eyebrows. Abbie shuddered and looked away from him. Nessa cocked her jaw and narrowed her eyes. Quick as lightning, her arm shot out and her fingers gripped Abbie's jaw hard, jerking her head to the right, and then the left. "What's he see in you, human girl? What makes you so special?" She leaned forward and drew Abbie's scent deep into her lungs. "Christ," she sneered, "you still smell like him. He probably fucked you just a few hours ago, didn't he?"

Abbie shrank back from the woman's resentment, but not quick enough. All at once, Nessa's hand came out and slapped her, so hard her ears rang. Stars exploded before her eyes. She fell back and was about to go down when Elijah caught her and jerked her back to her feet with a vicious tug on her restraints.

"Knock it off, Nessa," he growled, holding Abbie up with one arm. "She's still got marks from that fuck-up Issac, she doesn't need any more beatings."

"Fuck you," she bit out angrily. "The little whore doesn't need your protection. Do you think I'm going to let her fuck Jaxon into making her his mate?"

Elijah snorted. "God you're a dumb bitch."

Suddenly Nessa screamed furiously, her hands reaching to scratch his eyes out. He laughed pulling Abbie behind his back and still managed to keep Nessa away with one arm.

"Knock it off, you bitch." He pushed her lightly and she fell back, only to spring to her feet and charge toward him again. Grabbing her by the hair violently, he threw her to the ground and smiled evilly. "I said," he enunciated clearly, "knock it off."

He turned to Abbie, and she saw his eyes changed and inhuman, pale yellow and spooky. "And you, Jaxon wants you ready in the barn."

"If he's going to fuck her, I want to fuck her!" Nessa sat up, blood dripping from a gash on her chin.

"He may or may not," he said lazily. "But she dies either way. She saw him eating some bitch on a road a couple of years back. Don't know why he didn't knock her off then."

Nessa wiped her face with the back of her hand, spreading blood along her cheek.

"I don't care. I want her first. I want her now!"

"You said she wanted Harley." Abbie's eyes went back and forth between them. She was about to meet the thing that caused her father's death, but she couldn't even focus on that while faced with these two. She looked harder and harder between them, trying to decide who was the greater threat, but she couldn't do it. Nessa was batshit crazy, but Elijah's maniacal hilarity was just as dangerous.

"No," he drawled, "I said she wanted the power fucking him would give her. I don't think she even likes dick."

"Give her to me," she ordered, her hands out, her fingers curled like claws. Elijah folded his arms across his chest, forgetting Abbie for a minute. "I want to watch."

Abbie didn't think twice. She shoved her shoulder into the small of the big man's back, turned around, and began running for her life. Her feet couldn't move fast enough as she heard Nessa laugh at the sky, the sound more of a high-pitched bark, and Elijah's bellow and snort as he joined the chase.

She headed for the trees, knowing it would be no contest and figuring the cover would help. She couldn't get away, but she could try to make one of them angry enough to kill her outright. Death didn't scare her however rape and torture did. She ducked between trees, dodged around bushes, and zigzagged as much as possible. She looked behind her saw no one, looked again, and saw the flash of a dark hide. Her heart immediately plummeted they'd changed their skins. Everything suddenly jerked to a halt as she tripped over a tree branch and fell onto her chest, so hard her breath whooshed out. Nothing moved for a second, and then the woods exploded. One landed on her back, heavy claws digging into her flesh. She screamed and tried to buck it off, but the creature stayed, already growling, and drooling on her neck.

"Little bitch," Nessa said gutturally. Abbie shuddered beneath her, ready to try and kick her when another form came from the woods and plowed into the female Were. They went tumbling, and Abbie didn't wait around. She clumsily got to her feet and started running again, the sounds of their fighting drowning out the heavy pounding of her heart.

Twenty seconds before she saw another flash of dark in the pale morning light. This time, it didn't come from behind, but from the side, and Abbie was forced to veer right. Only then did she see the other Were, already waiting. It pounced, and she went down.

It snarled, its cock hanging out, red and ridged, ready to rip her apart. Elijah's laugh came from the animal's throat, deeper and far more terrifying than before.

"Pretty bitch," he said through growls. "Gonna eat you up." His clawed hand ripped at her shirt and scratched her breasts. She tried to twist away, only to be stopped by Nessa, who stood ready at the side, a wide gash open along her stomach. She panted and drooled as she stared at them. *"Give me a tasssste..."*

Elijah snarled back at her and leaped off, guarding Abbie with a snap of his muzzle. Nessa jumped away, then circled and rushed him, locking onto his hind leg, tearing, and clawing at him. They fell, both dominant and strong, and

Abbie huddled against the snow, trying to get air into her lungs as she watched the horror play out in front of her.

They were evenly matched, she thought, turning on her side and watching through glazed eyes. Elijah was larger, but Nessa was nastier, and in the end, with her muzzle coated in blood, she ripped his eye out with one swipe of her claws, and Elijah was left bleeding heavily, gasping through the pain as he fell aside.

"Now," Nessa said, slinking over to Abbie with her breath puffing out, "I'll have my taste."

Abbie kicked at her and connected solidly with her muzzle. Nessa's head snapped to the side, a sharp bark of pain escaping from her throat. When she turned back, her body trembled with rage. Her lips lifted in a warning snarl, and then she struck, latching onto Abbie's calf, her teeth sinking into her flesh. She felt nothing except the intense pressure of the creature's jaw. She held her for a moment, then jerked her entire body. Nessa dropped Abbie's leg and fell back, howling.

CHAPTER 27

Abbie's breath froze in her chest as she watched her. The creature's head lowered again as her tongue came out and cleaned her muzzle. She eyed Abbie like a juicy roast, then her body collected, readying to strike. Abbie tried to steady herself, and when Nessa lunged, she closed her eyes and waited for the pain to start. It never came.

A new snarl, this one deeper and meaner, echoed in the woods. Abbie opened her eyes and inched back, staring as Harley leaped onto Nessa, his hands deadly with claws, ripping her apart with little effort. She growled and changed her attack, aiming for him, only to be caught mid-leap, her head clenched between his hands. With one quick twist, her neck was broken. Harley roared and threw her to the side like trash.

"Come on!"

Abbie flinched away, but it was Killian, bending down and hurriedly lifting her in his arms. "We need to leave, right now."

He ran from the woods with her clutched to his chest, looking behind him every few seconds. She couldn't help but stare at the massacre that was Harley as he opened Elijah's body from pelvis to neck with a vicious roar. Elijah put up a little fight and died, blood streaming from his empty eye socket and his intestines spilling from his open abdomen.

"Don't watch," Killian ordered sharply, stopping next to the Bronco, and shoving her in the passenger side.

Cormac was there behind the wheel, revving the engine. "Come on! He's already on the chase."

Another roar shook the forest this one contained so much ragged pain forcing birds to flee their branches.

"Go," Killian gritted out jumping in behind Abbie and pulling the door. Cormac threw the vehicle in gear, and they roared off, leaving the old farm behind. Abbie watched out the back as it grew smaller and smaller.

The drive seemed to take forever, when they stopped the car, neither of the men moved. "What's wrong?" she asked.

"Shhh." Killian held his hand up, quieting her. Then after a minute of silence, he said softly, "Shit," and threw his door open.

He helped Abbie out just as Cormac came around, ready to help.

"He's close," Killian said, picking her up and running to the front door. Ryan was there, holding it open and motioning them inside with a desperate wave, yelling, "Hurry!"

As soon as they were in, he slammed the door shut, locked it, and shoved three deadbolts home. Abbie watched through glazed eyes as he tugged over a huge trunk and started piling bags of what looked like sand against the door.

"What's wrong?" she asked groggily. "Why are you acting like we're about to be attacked?"

Ryan added more bags, stacking them until they nearly covered the door. "Go take care of her," he said, heaving another bag over. "Cormac and I can finish this."

"Let me know if he tries to come through," Killian ordered. He took her through the living room, staying away from the windows, and carried her upstairs. As he set her on the bed Abbie rolled to her stomach.

"Can you loosen my hands?"

Killian went to the bathroom and came back with scissors. Once the bands were broken from her wrists, it took a few minutes before her circulation came back. When it did, the pain was worse than anything she'd experienced. She couldn't help but cry as her nerves tingled back to life.

"Christ, you're all messed up," Killian muttered. He got a towel from the bathroom and pressed it to her wrists. "Hold still. I'll be right back."

He was gone a minute before returning with his medical supplies. He already had the bandages and gauze pulled out, and immediately set to work, cleaning up her wrists and applying antibiotic ointment.

"It's ugly more than anything," he said, peering into the wounds around her wrists. She looked away and gritted her teeth until it was done.

After her wrists were bandaged, he looked at her back, which was heavily bruised more than anything, and then at her leg, which wasn't nearly as bad as she'd feared. There were two puncture wounds, but they were clean and relatively small. The worst of the damage was heavy bruising, which went up nearly to her knee.

"Well, at least we don't need to worry about rabies," he quipped, taping a bandage over the wound, his eyes going to the window for a second before returning to her leg.

"You'll heal."

Glancing at the window, she asked, "What's wrong?" Just then, the cry of a lone wolf cut the night. "Harley," she whispered, answering her question. He nodded.

He was close, close enough she knew she could see him if she looked out the window in the living room. His howl was long and lonely, and sad, she thought. It broke off, and then there was a minute of silence. When a heavyweight hit the house, making the walls vibrate from the force, Killian hung his head and whispered, "Shit."

She stood up and whirled in a circle, trying to decide which side he was hitting.

"What's he doing?" she asked in a hushed voice.

"He's trying to get you," he said, following her nervous movements. "He fought for you and won and now he wants you as his prize."

"Wants me how?"

He stared at her, his eyes glittering. "He wants you in his pelt. He wants to mate. It's embedded in us like in other species that fight for mates. That's why we got you out of there. He didn't want to have to take you like that because he can't help himself."

"Oh, God." She leaned against the wall for a minute, absorbing the idea. Harley was dominant and aggressive as a man. She couldn't even think about what he'd be like in his changed form.

"He's not going for the windows. Why?" she asked, as another hit rocked the house.

"They're specially made, reinforced. A bullet couldn't even get through those windows, and he knows it, so he's aiming elsewhere, hoping to break through."

The house shook again from the force of his body. Ryan came running up the stairs panting. "He's trying to get through the south walls."

Killian surged up. "Dammit!" he said, and they both left the bedroom. Abbie felt the vibrations of another hit, and her body shuddered along with the house. The south wall would be the living room, or maybe the study. Actually, it was the direction their shared bedroom faced. That's where he was trying to come through.

After a minute, silence reigned again, and she couldn't help but hold her breath, expecting another hit with every second that passed. Needing something to do, she undressed and used a washcloth to wipe away the worst dirt. Afterward, she pulled on her sweats and stood by the window, needing to see. There was hardly anything to see trees, snow, and darkness. The sun wasn't up yet, and she realized it wasn't even mid-morning. It seemed funny to think she would have been eating breakfast with Killian right now if not for the mess she'd created.

From the trees a huge, black form easily visible against the snow, its body covered in thick hair the color of midnight. It ran, increasing its speed until it was nothing more than a blurred shadow, and crashed into the side of the house. Abbie couldn't see the damage he was causing, but from the shaking of the structure, it had to be substantial. Pieces of siding already littered the snow as evidence of his previous efforts.

She turned away from the window and winced. Her calf hurt every time she put weight on it. It was strong enough to use, but the pain made it difficult as she walked downstairs to find the men. They were all in the kitchen, standing around the counter, their eyes wary and their bodies tense.

"I'm sorry," she said as she joined them. Tears burned her eyes, but she fought against them and tried to keep a brave face. "I'm so sorry. I didn't know what else to do except run."

Killian sighed and dragged her into his arms, burying his nose in her hair. "It's not your fault, love. You're young and impetuous, and we've forced you to accept major changes in your life."

"Is he going to break in?" she asked against his shirt. He didn't answer right away. "I don't know," he said truthfully. "I've never seen him like this and he's strong. This house is supposed to be safe, but…" He shrugged and left it at that.

"Will he kill me if I go out there?"

"You're not going out," he automatically replied, tightening his arms around her.

"He asked me to keep you in until the rut leaves him."

The house shuddered again, then again. There was silence for a minute, and then another long howl. Ryan's eyes closed, and an almost dreamy look came over his face. She watched him, realizing he wanted to be out there, running wild with his brother.

The house settled around them, each too nervous to speak in case the noise attracted him again.

"What happens if he gets in any way?"

"Then we're all fucked," Ryan said bluntly, his eyes opening.

"I'll go out," she said quietly.

"She should," Cormac said immediately, only to flinch from Killian's answering snarl.

Abbie put her hand on his chest and pushed away from him. "I made this mess. If it takes me going out there and dealing with him to fix it…" She sighed. "I'm terrified, but I don't want you to get hurt protecting me."

"We'll wait," Ryan said. "We'll see if he's going to bust through. If it looks like he's going to, you can go out. But not before, Abs. He's lethal right now. He wouldn't kill you, but..." He shrugged, leaving the rest to her imagination. Unfortunately, she had a vivid imagination, and all sorts of images popped into her head, not all of them distasteful, which worried her almost as much as Harley.

Killian nodded in agreement. "We'll wait, preferably in the living room so I can drink. Abbie, be careful with your leg. I don't want you making the wound worse."

He stayed at her side as she hobbled to the living room, forcing her to take the chair nearest him. After she was seated, he elevated her damaged leg on pillows before seating himself and pouring a large whiskey. For a few minutes, nothing was said as they all waited on edge and jumpy. Then Harley hit again, and the house shook. Every time he hit the house, Ryan flinched, looked over his shoulder toward the window, and muttered, "Fuck." Cormac just shook his head and looked sympathetic. The time passed slowly. Killian attempted to read, Ryan and Cormac played chess, and Abbie sat in her chair and stared out the window. The attempts to break in got more desperate as the afternoon progressed and finally in a frantic two-hour period of almost solid hits against the house, it stopped completely.

"It's been an hour since he's done anything," Ryan said, glancing at the clock as he moved his bishop. "He's over it."

"I don't know," Cormac said, moving his queen forward. "I wouldn't put it past him to stop just to get you to open the door."

"We wait," Killian said sharply, looking over the top of his book. "When he's all right, we'll know."

At quarter to twelve, he knocked on the door.

CHAPTER 28

Killian went to let him in and took a step back at his appearance. "My God, are you all right?"

Harley brushed past him; his eyes still changed but the rest of him back to normal. He did not answer as he stalked into the house and went to the kitchen. He pulled a glass down, filled it with water, and drank it in one gulp. He refilled the glass twice more before he was satisfied.

"Where is she?" he asked through gritted teeth, his hands clenching on the rim of the sink.

"Harley," he said cautiously. "She didn't mean to hurt you."

"I'm here," she answered, limping to the doorway and staring at him. He was nude and covered in dark bruises and cuts. They almost his entire body. His head turned toward her slowly. "Get upstairs."

She opened her mouth and looked to Killian for help.

"No!" Harley flew at her, pinning her against the wall with his body. "You will obey me in this, or I'll fuck you right here!"

She stared at him, fear lancing her body. Gulping, she nodded her head. "All right."

He released her and she slid across the wall toward the steps, her movements slow and painful, like an old woman with arthritis.

"Harley," Killian tried again.

"Don't tell me how to treat her," he said sharply, staring at the steps where she'd disappeared.

"She's young," Killian cautioned carefully. "She didn't leave to hurt you. Be careful with her, Harley."

"Stay out of it." With one last look, he left the kitchen and climbed the stairs, his cock already hard for her.

She couldn't make herself get into the bed. For one thing, she was sure she was going to be ill the moment he stepped through the door and wanted to be ready to run to the bathroom if needed. For another, he was already at his peak of rage. She wasn't risking anything by not being in bed, so she stayed near the window and waited. She tried not to think about the other emotion running rampant, but it was there all the same, and nearly as strong as the fear. *Guilt.* The sucker of all emotions and possibly the most damaging.

He came into the room silently, closing and locking the door behind him. He was already aroused and ready as he stopped next to her and jerked her hands up for his inspection. He stared at her bandaged wrists for a second and then dropped them without a word. With stiff movements, he pulled and pushed until her sweats lay in a pile on the floor, and she was as nude as he was.

"What are you doing?" she asked, staring up at him fearfully. He crowded her against the wall, using his chest and arms as a cage. She leaned back against the wall, her stomach plummeting.

"You ran from me," he bit out, sliding his hips closer to her until he was pinning her lower body to the wall. "You ran away from me!" He breathed hard as he faced her, his eyes still wild.

She looked away and tried to ignore the feel of him against her, so large and hard. She would have missed the feel of him his scent. It would have hurt to be separated from him. "I needed to get away for a little while."

"You're a fucking liar," he snapped, abruptly stepping away from her and going to the bed. "Did you think I'd let you leave?" His head cocked to the side, his eyes staring at her, already fucking her. "Did you think you could get away from me?" he sneered.

"Yes," she said honestly.

He inhaled sharply, his anger growing from her answer. "Get on the fucking bed."

She got on the bed and lay down, stiff as a board.

He crawled to her, his muscles shifting unnaturally, as inhuman as his eyes. She realized how close he was to changing again and vowed to do everything he told her. He jerked her legs apart. "I'm going to lick your pussy, baby. I'm going to drink all that juice out of your pussy and make you cum again and again until you're begging for my cock. And you will beg, do you understand?"

She gave a brief nod and inhaled, shuddering.

He pulled one of her legs over his shoulder and went at her as if she was a meal and he was starving. His tongue licked her all over, starting at the bottom and going all the way up to her clit. Every fold of skin was touched, examined, and then licked again. He went as deep as he could go, tongue-fucking her through an orgasm, and then moved up and sucked her clit until she had another. He did it over and over, wringing climax after climax from her, in between drawing her juices out and drinking them down. Then he'd return and make her orgasm again.

He went on forever, without giving her recovery time, forcing her to take it. As she became more and more sensitive, he began to use his teeth, biting her clit gently, which sent her spinning and made her scream and lose her breath. After, he used his fingers and began thrusting them deep into her while he nibbled at her outer lips. She was so sensitive all over she nearly came from it, but he held back, biting at her inner thigh for a minute while she cooled down. Then he went back to her pussy and did it all over again.

It went on and on. She lost count of how many times she came, but with each one, her body felt emptier and emptier, as if he were licking her soul away and eating it down with her heat. By the time the clock struck two, she felt as boneless as a rag doll and just as lifeless.

"Harley," she whispered hoarsely, his name coming out as a plea. He raised his head; his eyes still Were, and his lips twisted in a snarl. "Please." She pulled at his shoulders. He thrust his fingers back into her pussy and lowered his mouth to her clit, becoming more forceful with his tongue.

She stiffened, and with a cry, came. "Harley, please!" She shuddered, wanting more, needing to be filled.

"Tell me what you want," he urged roughly, coming up over her, still pushing his fingers inside her.

"Anything," she gasped, arching to get closer to him, but it did no good. She wanted his body against hers, his chest, his legs, his stomach. She wanted to feel his body heat and the smoothness of his skin. But he held himself away from her and watched her writhing, a bitter smile on his lips. He didn't touch her except where his hand was buried deep within her.

"Tell me you want my cock, Abbie. Tell me you want it deep."

"I do. Please, Harley. Please I need you inside me."

He leaned closer and whispered against her lips. "Promise you'll never leave me, Abbie. Promise it, and I'll fuck you."

She nodded, her hands holding his head still to kiss him. "I won't," she whispered against his lips, urging him to respond, but he held still as her tongue flitted over his mouth. "I'll never leave you," she promised, then sucked in a deep breath as he jerked her leg over his shoulder and forced his cock into her, all at once. She screamed from the shock of the invasion, but her hips immediately picked up his rhythm and joined him there.

"More," she panted, squeezing her inner muscles around him. He thrust harder, grunting each time, his pace quickening until it was inhumanly fast, the piston movements of his hips sharp and punctuated.

Neither of them lasted long. She came with a cry at the same time he did. He hissed and flooded her body with his seed. She tightened her loose leg around his hips and tried to hold him inside her. She looked deep into his eyes and saw all the pain there, the pain she'd caused.

He only gave her a minute before he began moving again, pushing in jerkily. "Take it," he gritted out and pulled her leg tighter against him as he continued. "I want you again."

She sucked in the air as she tried to fight her body's ultra-sensitivity. She needed a break from the sensory overload, but he rode her through it, his face twisted with anger and lust and bitter hurt, forcing her to accept him and his attentions. He took her through two more orgasms, flipping her to her stomach for one, then afterward making her stand so he could take her against the wall. She cried through it, imploring him to let her rest, but he was relentless, and her body it wanted to cum, no matter what her mind said.

"Do you know how good your body holds me?" he taunted against her ear, breathing hard with every plunge of his cock. "It's the tightest little pussy I've ever felt, and it's all mine, Abbie. All mine. I'll never let you leave me, do you understand?"

His words pushed her over the edge, and with the next orgasm, her body didn't recover. It stayed ready at the peak, just waiting for one more time. Feeling her readiness, he slid his hand down to her clit, and with each penetration, his fingers had an answering motion against her hot flesh.

She came again, so hard and fast her vision wavered for an instant, her heart nearly bursting from the rioting sensations. He thrust three times more before he came, the last push of his hips so strong it brought her feet off the floor and pinned her to the wall. His body shook against her, and his cock seemed to jump inside her as it spurted, covering her womb with seed.

When he pulled out, her legs gave, and she crumpled to the floor.

"Saddle-sore?" he asked sardonically, with one eyebrow raised, a mean twist on his lips.

She pushed herself up on shaking legs. She watched him warily he was still furious. She fell against the wall, barely managing to conceal a moan of pain. He reached out for her, and she recoiled from him. "Don't."

His hand dropped to his side, his accent was suddenly crisp and hard. "Then get into the shower, if you can."

She turned her head away from him and pushed against the wall, determined to make it to the bathroom unaided. She managed to stand upright, her legs screaming in protest, but wasn't able to take that first step, and after a minute she tipped to the side until her shoulder was once again leaning against the wall.

"Stupid fool." He scooped her up and carried her to the bathroom, his jaw clenched and his eyes sparkly, like cold emeralds. "It'd serve you right if I left you in there, too weak to even help yourself."

"I'm fine," she said, refusing to look at him. But she held onto him, her arms tight around his neck as he carried her.

He sat her on the toilet and pulled her chin in his hand, forcing her to stare at him. "Don't fuck with me," he growled, rubbing his thumb across her kiss-swollen bottom lip. "You owe me big for this last stunt, and I'm going to collect."

She jerked her chin from his hand. His fingers loosened and let her go, but she knew it was because he chose to.

He turned the shower on, adjusted the temperature, and crooked his finger at her.

"Get in."

She held out her wrists. "I need these off first."

CHAPTER 29

Although he appeared cruel when he removed her bandages, his hands were all gentleness. For some reason, it made her cry as she stepped into the shower. After five minutes, she was shaking too much to stand. He pulled her against his body, and she rested against him thankfully, taking comfort from his strength. He cleaned her with a soft rag and copious amounts of soap, careful around any new cuts and bruises. He washed her back, her stomach, her breasts, and between her legs, being especially careful there. She was still sensitive and jerked against him from the soft abrasion of the cloth.

She held onto him as the shower beat down on them, the warm spray doing wonders for her body and aching muscles. "Thank you," she whispered, moving closer to him and hanging onto his shoulders, needing the feel of him against her, strong and dependable. "Thank you for finding me. Thank you for not letting them get me."

He didn't say anything, but he held her and rubbed her back as she cried. When they got out, he dried her off just as carefully, and then carried her to bed. She watched him go back to the bathroom and then come out with a bottle of oil, which he set on the table near the bed.

"You're not done," he said coolly as he joined her on the bed, pulling her body toward him. "Now, spread your legs."

She was going to refuse him and was about to do so when his hand pulled her thighs apart, widening them. He left her like that for a second, and then his hands were back, rubbing lightly over her inner thighs, spreading warm oil over her skin. He seemed content with just rubbing her thighs for a while but gradually, his hands moved farther and farther in, until he was working the oil into her folds, rubbing her delicately with his callused and scarred hands, as if she were a piece of spun glass. She couldn't help the heat that started to grow to life in the pit of her stomach, but she resented it. She resented how her hips angled for him, making his petting easier, and resented the fact that she could still get hot, even after the multiple orgasms her body already had.

"You're so soft," he marveled, tracing a finger down her slit and the tip rim lightly. "And pretty. So pink, so lovely."

She bit her lip to keep from moaning, but her hips betrayed her and tilted up, searching for his finger, wanting more depth.

"Is this what you want?" he murmured, letting his finger sink into her several times before pulling it out.

Her head thrashed on the pillow as she fought the desire for him. What had she become? Because of this man, she couldn't control her reactions or her body's unstoppable needs.

He leaned down and licked her pussy, groaning against her clit as his tongue dug into her deeply. "I can taste myself on you, Abbie," he purred letting his tongue burrow into her further.

She cried out as her body clenched around his invading tongue. It was hot and slick, but she needed more.

His tongue flicked upward, paying homage to her clit before he clamped down on it and sucked the nub of flesh. She jerked beneath him, her body needing completion.

"Want more?" he asked, raising his head and letting his finger push into her again. She didn't say anything, and just breathed heavily with her head turned away.

"You have to say it," he growled at her. "Tell me you want my cock, Abbie."

Tears fell down her cheeks, burning across her skin. "I want your cock, Harley."

It came out as nothing more than a whisper, but it was enough. Carefully, he lifted her hips and positioned his cock at her entrance, pushing forward so slowly that she mewled with it. When he was halfway in, he surged forward until he was fully seated, stopping for a minute and just breathing in her scent.

"So tight," he marveled, pulling out and sliding back smoothly. "God your pussy is tight."

He held himself up with one arm, and let the other caress her breasts, using his fingers to pluck at her nipples, to make them peak and beg for his attention. She cried out, arching closer to his hand. Still thrusting, he leaned down and took one into his mouth, sucking hard in time with his thrusts, flicking his tongue over the bud. So gently he moved, every motion of his hips was smooth and slow. It drove her crazy, she needed to cum. The need was there, like before, just as strong, just waiting. But he kept denying her, keeping his penetration shallow and lazy the closer she got. Although her orgasm built slowly, she was held at the top for a long time. She breathed heavily with her eyes squeezed shut as he sucked on her nipples and played with her clit. When she was ready to scream, needing to cum so bad she was going mad, he finally dug his cock in all the way, sharply and violently, sending her over the edge on a piercing shriek.

She came down with no memory of him coming, but she could tell he had. She was wet with it and could feel it flooding her core. He was still leaning over her, propped up by his elbow with his hand caressing her breast.

He leaned down and kissed her deeply, letting her taste herself on his tongue and in his mouth. When he pulled back, his eyes flashed at her, full of foreboding. "If you ever run from me again, Killian won't be there to protect you. You'll have to take me, in the change, and I'll fuck you until you can't move. Do you understand me?"

She nodded.

CHAPTER 30

She was lethargic and morose when she woke at midday. She didn't get up. Her body was too heavy like it sensed the tension in the house and prepared for it accordingly by making movement hard. She hadn't even stepped out of the bedroom, but she could feel the strain in the air. She stayed in bed as long as she could and went downstairs for dinner.

She knew she looked terrible as she walked into the kitchen, and it was reinforced by the double take Killian did when he saw her.

"Are you all right?" He came around the counter, wiping his hands on a towel, and helped her to a stool.

"I'm fine," she lied. "Where's Harley?" She needed to know that. To know he was close.

Killian nodded his head toward the study. "In there, doing some research on his latest commission. Do you want me to get him?"

"No."

He stood away from her, studying her form. She was pale, her hair limp, and she looked like she was about to fall over. He wasn't one to worry incessantly, but her appearance was enough to cause concern, that, and the difference in her scent. Just to double-check, he inhaled deeply when he stood next to her it was there, a subtle change, but a change all the same.

"Why don't I get you some coffee, and then we'll look at your wounds, hmm?" He filled a mug, added plenty of sugar, and handed it to her. She took it and held it with two hands while he went off for his medical bag. She set her mug aside when he returned and held out both her hands.

After cleaning and bandaging the lacerations, he went back to preparing dinner. He kept it simple and prepared a meatloaf, all the while looking over his shoulder at Abbie to make sure she was still sitting up.

Dinner was uncomfortable. No one spoke, which was bad enough, but Harley seemed set on being as overbearing and demanding as he could possibly be, staring at her woodenly throughout the meal, and frowning as she picked at her food. She became so uncomfortable she kept her eyes pasted to the tablecloth.

"She's not to leave the house until I've taken care of Jaxon," he said, turning to Killian. "She can't be trusted not to run, and she's too vulnerable outside."

"Harley, stop it," he said, his eyes gleaming in warning. "She's suffered enough. There's no point in torturing her."

"She's mine," he bit out, turning his head toward her. "Apparently that's all the reason he needs to take her."

She choked and coughed as a pea lodged in her throat, the memory of Elijah's taunting ringing through her ears. Ryan pounded her on the back until she held her hand out, begging him to stop.

"That's not why he took me," she gasped, reaching for her water and drinking it down.

"Are you going to tell us how you know of him?" Killian asked, setting his fork down. "I'm assuming you don't object to his dying after this last episode. Elijah was Jaxon's cousin. There's no doubt about the connection this time."

She finished her water and set the glass aside. She bowed her head and played with the napkin on her lap, not sure how to start. "I did first hear that name at the pub. You guys were discussing him at the table."

"But that's not why you asked about him," Harley said sharply. She shook her head. "No. I heard his name from Issac, the night he shot Ryan. He spoke of Jaxon."

Harley leaned back in his chair lazily, but she wasn't stupid enough to ignore the menace in his cool gaze. "Really?" he murmured.

Killian watched him for a second before turning back to Abbie. "And you still didn't tell us? Why?"

"Jaxon didn't tell that man to hurt me," she said lamely. "He just wanted him to take me somewhere. I knew you were going to kill him when I told you, so I didn't."

"Foolish little girl," Harley spat. "He almost killed you."

"But then Elijah talked about him too," she continued, wrapping the napkin around her fingers tight enough to make the tips purple. "And he admitted Jaxon wanted me dead."

Killian nodded. "So now you tell us," he murmured. "Lass, he's like that. He's the type of man who takes advantage of anything he can. He wants you dead for no other reason than to hurt Harley. It's not fair to you, but that's how Jaxon operates."

She lifted her head. "You've got it wrong. He wants me for a different reason, at least according to Elijah he does."

"What could he possibly want you for?" Ryan asked, frowning. "He doesn't even know you."

"Actually, he does. He's the—"

"—Were you saw the night your father died," Killian finished for her, realization dawning.

She nodded. "Yes. At first, I wondered if it were true, but if it weren't, how would he even know what I saw?"

Silence reigned for a few minutes. "He's been gone for a few years," Ryan said finally, propping his chin on his hand. "And no one seems to know exactly where he was. The only answer I ever got was in the States somewhere."

"When did he return to the area?" Harley asked.

"I don't know." Ryan shrugged. "Maybe a month ago."

After another minute of silence, Killian said, "So you can call him out before the full moon." He looked at Harley and nodded slowly. "He killed a woman as prey. You have a witness to testify to that. That's all you need."

Ryan whistled. "That's heavy stuff, though. You better be pretty sure about everything before you announce it to the pack. There're going to be some who object to the charge."

"You can have Abbie speak," he argued, tapping his finger on the table for emphasis. "Any member of the pack will be able to scent a lie."

Harley's eyes went from Ryan to Killian, finally settling on Abbie. "Ryan, call Cormac and tell him. I want this fucker out of commission within a week."

Ryan pushed his chair back and nodded. "Right." He headed to the den to use the phone.

Harley left the table, calling over his shoulder, "She's to stay in the house until this is finished."

"Where are you going?" Killian frowned at his back.

Harley yanked the door open. "For a run."

Late that night, Abbie fell asleep to the sound of howls echoing through the woods. She had nightmares.

The next morning, she felt even worse. It was bad enough she sat on the toilet with her head in her hands, ready in case she needed to throw up. Nothing came of it except an hour of true misery, and Harley's large form, frowning as he stood in the doorway.

"Go away," she whispered.

"You're ill?" He leaned down and pressed his hand to her cheek. "You don't feel warm."

"Just go away," she said again, rolling her eyes up at him. "The last thing I need right now is for you and your insults to witness my utter humiliation as I throw up in the toilet. Please, Harley."

He leaned in closer and inhaled sharply. She thought about pushing his head away, but it would require too much effort, so she ignored him, even when he jerked back, his eyes suddenly wide as he stared down at her.

"I'm going to get Killian."

She groaned but let him leave, happy just to be by herself in the cool bathroom. It was surprising how much of a comfort the cooler temperature was. She'd never been in a position to suffer through nausea. Usually, she just vomited up whatever was in her stomach immediately. But, this time, she had time to think through it and analyze what made the nausea worse, and what made it better. All in all, she preferred the instant vomiting the absence of suffering was extremely appealing. Connor came rushing into the room, his silky striped pajamas perfect on his sleep-tumbled form. Even his beard seemed slightly mussed, she thought as she stared up at him.

All businesslike, he dampened a washcloth with cold water and held it to her forehead. "God, that feels good," she moaned, leaning into the coolness of it.

"We'll do this for a minute, then I'm taking you downstairs and we'll see if we can't get some tea and saltines into you. That may help."

She didn't argue with him, too happy with the washcloth to bother. As it turned out, the tea and crackers did help, and an hour later, she was feeling fine. With renewed energy, she went back to the bedroom to change and prepare for her morning.

Harley was still in bed, lying on top of the covers with his body stretched out and taking up three-fourths of the bed. She admired him for a minute before going to the dresser and pulling out her clothes for the day.

"You're feeling better?"

She made a noncommittal noise.

"I mean it," he murmured. "You stay in the house."

She paused in the act of pulling her jeans on. "I understand."

He turned over onto his back and watched as she finished dressing. She blushed through it, but she didn't rush away and hide, figuring that he'd seen everything there was to see already. Except for any vomiting, thank God.

"I know I said this last night, but thank you for coming to find me," she whispered, as she tugged a shirt over her head. She kept her back turned to him as she said it, not wanting to see his face tighten with anger at the reminder.

"Why'd you leave?"

She thought for a minute to organize her reasons before she answered. "I don't ever want to be the cause of another person's death." She pulled the shirt down over her stomach.

"Even if he threatens your life?" he questioned, propping himself up on an elbow.

"I tried to end my life," she pointed out, looking at him over her shoulder. "That's not a very good argument."

"Then why now?" he asked, his tone becoming rough. "Why tell us about him now?"

"He killed that woman."

He swore and fell back on the bed, covering his eyes with his arm. "I don't understand you."

"Then we're even," she replied, walking over and sitting beside him on the bed.

"Because I don't understand you either."

CHAPTER 31

After the first day of being cooped up, she was ready to rip her hair out. She was surprised at how accustomed she'd become to going around the property as she pleased, taking walks along the trails, visiting the barns, and even helping shovel snow. She'd become accustomed to the physical activity, and now her body craved it. She'd spent the first half of the day in the study, drawing. When she stood back and looked at the finished product, she realized the Were was Harley and not her monster of nightmares.

She shook her head over it but put the picture aside for later. By midday, after going through her normal routine of activities, she needed something different, and she went in search of Killian. He was in the kitchen, baking and looking like one of those serious baking people the cooking shows always raved about.

"Can I at least shovel off the porch?" she asked.

"No." He pulled a pan from the oven and set it aside, examining it as critically as if it were one of his paintings. She leaned on the counter and sighed. "I need something to do. Like right now, or I'm going to go insane."

"You've done that already," he quipped. "Choose something a little more original."

She pursed her lips in thought and pictured the drawing of Harley. "Has Harley ever posed for you nude?"

He dropped the pan he was holding and stared at her like she had two heads. "Nude? Harley?" He propped his hand on his hip and shook his head, marveling at her. "Do you realize how much stronger you've become since you've been here? You never would have asked me a question like that a few weeks ago."

"I'm not sure if that's a good thing," she said, slouching slightly. "So, has he?"

He bent down and picked up the pie pan, setting it in the sink as he turned on the tap. "Harley doesn't do nude."

She thought about that for a minute before attempting to put the idea away. But it was difficult she couldn't quite get the image of him out of her head.

Cormac stopped by later in the afternoon. Killian ushered him into the house and led him to the kitchen.

"Abbie," he said, pouring a cup of coffee and handing it to Cormac, "would you please call Harley and tell him Cormac is here? The number's beside the phone."

Her eyes flew to Cormac for a second and then she nodded. When she rang him, she said simply, "Cormac is here."

He sighed on the other end. "I'll be over."

When she returned to the kitchen, Ryan had joined the other two men and sat beside Cormac at the counter. She leaned against the doorway and zoned out as they discussed the problems that would arise from the charge. Cormac stayed through the evening and went over strategy and the wording of the official challenge with the men. Abbie tried to listen, but after a minute, her eyes started drooping. The next thing she knew, she was being carried up the steps.

"I'm sorry," she murmured against Harley's chest, wiggling closer. "I didn't mean to stop your meeting."

"We were done, and you're tired," he said.

He carried her to their bedroom and laid her on the bed, shaking his head when she tried to shed her clothes herself.

"Let me." He pushed her hands aside.

"Okay," she whispered, and let sleep take her.

She woke up early again, her stomach as unhappy as the day before. She sat on the floor of the bathroom for a half hour with a wet washcloth on her forehead. When she felt marginally better, she headed for the kitchen, where she served herself tea and crackers.

Ryan came down an hour later. She was so shocked she double-checked the clock just to make sure she wasn't mistaken about the time. He slumped onto a stool and leaned against the counter, bleary-eyed and ragged, with dark shadows under his eyes and his face covered in whiskers.

"Why are you up?" She searched his face for any sign of life, but there was little there. Ryan was one of those people who shouldn't be up before noon, much less eight in the morning.

His lids cracked open, revealing bloodshot eyes. Without prompting, she got him a cup of coffee, leaving it black. His tired flesh briefly lifted in a weak smile of thanks before he grasped the mug and held onto it for dear life. He seemed to go into a trance for fifteen minutes before he lifted the cup to his lips. After that, he began to wake, although, from the looks of it, it was a long and painful process.

"Better?" she asked, refilling his mug.

"Mmm." He sipped and winced from the hot liquid. "I feel like shit."

"You kind of look it, too." She studied him with a worried frown. "Do you want me to get you anything? Maybe an aspirin or something?"

"Yes," he groaned, holding his hand out desperately.

She got him the tablets and smiled as he looked at them as if they were God's gift before popping them in his mouth. He ignored the glass of water she'd set next to him and swallowed them dry. "Thank you."

She resumed her seat beside him and chewed on another cracker. "Want to tell me about it?"

"It's nothing serious, Abs," he sighed, opening his eyes fully for the first time. Absently, he snagged one of her crackers and popped it in his mouth, grimacing as he chewed. "Jesus, these are awful. Anyway, it's just Killian. He's getting nervous about the fight coming up. He always does this when Harley's going into a serious battle. I think he just went to sleep about an hour ago."

She motioned to the baked items lining the counters. It looked more like a bakery than a private home. "Is that why he's been doing all the baking?"

"It's how he copes," Ryan said. "He bakes and then I'm left to eat everything. I'm probably going to gain twenty pounds by the time the damn thing is over."

He sounded so morose over it, that she smiled. "Has Harley ever lost one?"

"No. But there's always that possibility. It's a brutal thing to watch the man you know as your brother rip the head off some guy you grew up with. The first time I saw him in battle, I was fourteen. I had nightmares for a month."

She flinched as his words dragged up the image of Harley killing Nessa and Elijah. It had been brutal, worse than anything she'd seen before.

"He's not like them," he said softly, reading her expression. "He'd never hurt anyone just to hurt them, and he's never drawn out the pain and torture because he could. Every kill he's made has been quick and clean. He's lethal, Abbie, but he isn't evil."

And that was the big difference, she supposed. He'd never hurt her, as angry as she'd made him, he'd never harmed her. He'd yelled, raged, and threatened, but he'd never done anything to suggest that he would ever do anything more than that. Frowning in thought, she stared at the counters and let the ugly thoughts and memories drift away. "Why is there nothing with chocolate?" she asked, straightening her spine and examining all the desserts. Her stomach clenched in hunger, and suddenly she needed chocolate.

"Brownies in the morning? What's wrong with you?" Killian frowned at her. A large pan of brownies sat in front of her, three rows already gone.

She ducked down slightly in embarrassment but still looked at the brownies greedily. "I'm sorry."

"And you, Ryan! I suppose you're part of this as well?" he huffed. Ryan shoved the last bite of his brownie in his mouth and chewed thoughtfully.

"She put tart cherries in them. Said it cut the too-much-chocolate thing. They're really good."

"It does," she said earnestly.

"Breakfast," Killian enunciated, "requires breakfast food. Namely eggs, cereal, bacon, fruit. Something of that nature." He pointed to the brownies with a shudder. "Those are not part of a morning meal. You realize, of course, that breakfast is the most important meal of the day, and look what you've wasted it on."

Lazily, Ryan reached over and pulled the pan toward him, cutting another large square and scooping it out with a wink and a smile. Abbie followed the brownie as if her eyes were physically attached to it.

"I can't believe this," Killian muttered with disgust, turning to the stove, and twisting the knob to the burner viciously, clearly vexed.

"If you were a nice person, you'd give me that brownie," Abbie said, sidling closer to Ryan.

He took a bite of it and said through the brownie, "I'm not a nice person."

She sighed and cut one for herself, slightly bigger than his. When she held it in her hand, all moist chocolate and frosting, she had a sudden feeling of satisfaction. Brownies were the underdog in the dessert world, completely underrated as a quality dessert.

And then it was plucked from her hand by a nasty old man with a temper. He whisked the brownie far away, several feet at least, and held it aloft as he scowled at her. "Go get dressed, Abbie. When you come back, I'll have a proper breakfast started."

"I need that," she pleaded, but he just shook his head.

"No, you've had enough. Now go."

She looked at him rebelliously for a minute, then at the pan still sitting on the counter, within reach.

"Don't even think about it."

She turned and stomped from the kitchen, her angry expression enough to let him know she was cursing him under her breath.

As soon as she was out of earshot, he turned on Ryan. "How could you? Don't you realize how delicate she is right now? She needs healthy food, not sweets!"

Ryan shrugged and took the brownie Killian still held in his hand. "Hey, she wanted chocolate. Who was I to stop her?"

"She's pregnant. The first months progress faster than a normal human pregnancy and she needs nutrition, not chocolate! You're going to be an uncle. Act like it!"

Ryan raised his hand in the air, like a student in elementary school. "Speaking of which, when is Harley going to tell her? And when is he going to marry her? Does he realize by human law his kid's last name is going to be Marsh unless he does the deed?"

Still irritated, Killian whipped out a pan and slapped it on the stove. "It's not my business to interfere in his relationship."

"Bullshit, old man try again, maybe something a little more believable?" he prodded.

Killian turned his head toward him and raised his brow. "Harley took my mother's ring to be sized."

Ryan halted in the act of biting his brownie and whistled. "Yup, that'll do it."

"It better...," he grumbled, cracking eggs into the pan.

CHAPTER 32

The tension in the house was palpable, thick enough to cut with a knife and serve with coffee. It would have been easy to use it as an excuse, but when she woke up nauseous and sick, again, she knew she had bigger problems to worry about than the anxiety the men were feeling. She was pregnant and so far it wasn't progressing normally, or at least she didn't think it was if she was experiencing morning sickness so early on. But then, Harley wasn't exactly human, so that kind of made sense.

"Fucking hell," she moaned, leaning her head against the cool tiles on the bathroom wall. It was even better than a cold washcloth. When one spot got too warm, she just slid her head over and she had a brand-new cold tile to use. She remembered her mother complaining about how sick she'd gotten when she was pregnant. It was always one of the complaints she issued as Abbie owed her for suffering through months of morning sickness. For the first time in her life, she felt a measure of compassion for her mother, because it was horrible. After a time, she got up and hurriedly dressed, making sure to be quiet so as not to wake Harley. She went downstairs after, anxious for the tea and crackers that seemed to be her cure-all. She wasn't sure what she was going to do. It was still a little early to take a pregnancy test, she thought since her period wasn't due for another week or so, but it did seem a little obvious. Of course, it wasn't all her fault. Harley was older and wiser at least he was supposed to be. It didn't negate her responsibility, however. She certainly should have thought about protection before she'd engaged in carnal activities and because she hadn't, she now had to suffer the consequences. It seemed her mother had been right after all.

Killian already had the pot on the stove and a cup prepared for her. She thanked him with a weak smile as she sat at the counter and pulled the box of crackers over, still trying to figure out what to do. She wasn't sure how Harley would react. He didn't seem like the type to be furious. Instead, she could easily picture him becoming even more protective and domineering. He'd make her life hell.

"You look sad," Killian commented.

She shrugged and bit into a cracker, chewing it slowly. After swallowing, she said, "I'll be fine." And she would be.

She slept through the afternoon. On the couch, no less.

She hadn't started out wanting a nap. She'd planned to page through a magazine, but the next thing she knew, she was cold and shaking, with images of sharp teeth coming at her. She woke up crying.

Killian came to the door of the kitchen, worry on his face. "Abbie?"

She sat up, heartsore and cold, looking around the room, slightly surprised to find herself in the living room. "Where's Harley?"

"The study lass, are you all right?"

She slid off the couch, her shoulders hunched as she wrapped her arms around her waist. "I'll be fine," she said over her shoulder, already heading for the study. Harley looked up from the papers on the desk when she pushed the door open and stepped in. His eyes were clouded as if he'd been focused entirely on what he was reading.

She didn't give him any time, not even to question her. She crawled into his lap and curled up around his neck. When his arms wrapped around her back and held her to him, she sighed and closed her eyes.

"I had the worst dream," she breathed. "Just awful."

"Did you?" He threw his pen down and nuzzled her hair. She nodded. "But I don't want to talk about it. I want to sit here for a little while... if that's okay."

He leaned back in the chair. "It's okay." He rocked gently. She closed her eyes and rested against him, absorbing his strength, his protection. It was funny to think that she'd never have met him if not for the loony bin, possibly the worst point in her life, yet it had given her so much. "You're a wonderful man, you know. Even though you try not to be."

"I'm glad you think so."

"I do." She smiled against his neck and let out a little sigh. "Harley, what is all this." She lifted her head from his shoulder and stared at the papers spread across the desk. They looked official, sort of. With stamps and seals, but none like she'd ever seen before.

He pulled a manila folder forward and handed it to her. His voice was devoid of emotion as he said, "These just arrived a while ago seems a pack in upstate New York had a problem with a rogue Alpha terrorizing the human population nearby. Four kills, each were blamed on a few of its members even though they knew it wasn't one of theirs."

She opened it and immediately gasped at the horror of the pictures inside. They were ghastly, the people in them torn into scraps of flesh and bone with blood splashed everywhere. She slammed the folder closed and threw it back on the desk. "Those are awful."

"Look at the last photo." He opened the folder and pulled the back picture to the front. It wasn't as grotesque as the others, but it was terrifying in its own right. A figure from her nightmares stood on it, his deep cooper fur easily identifiable under the garage light as he chewed on the arm of some poor soul. His eyes were just as empty as she remembered.

"That's him," she whispered. He replaced the picture and closed the folder, tossing it on the desk. "The pack leader is a man who used to run with us up here. He recognized Jaxon's scent, even though he'd met him just once before, this will add to the case against him."

She returned her head to his shoulder, the image in the picture made the one in her head solidify and match it. "Do I still have to go to your meeting?"

"Yes."

"And then you have to fight him." She didn't like that at all. "Aren't you worried?"

"I'm not stupid," he said softly, wielding the end of her braid like it was a paintbrush. He made one swipe, and then another against her cheek. "I know what I can take, and I can't, Abbie. I can take Jaxon." He dropped her braid and cupped her jaw with one hand, tilting her head so she looked into his eyes. "I do know."

"But have you ever met anyone you couldn't take before?"

"No." His eyes looked into hers, completely impassive.

"So, you don't know, then," she argued earnestly. "Harley," she grasped at his hand desperately, "this doesn't make me feel any better."

"You worried?"

"Well, you're going to be fighting a huge man-beast thing with really big claws and a terrible temper. They're going to be people watching and cheering, I suppose although I never did understand that part." She marveled over the brutality of man and Were for a second. "You're going to be trying to kill him, and he you. You should be worried, too."

He smiled slightly, just the barest curve of his lips. "Why should I, when you and Killian are doing it so well for me?"

"This isn't funny," she whispered.

He tilted his head and studied her. "No, it isn't. But it's how we settle charges like this. He is guilty you've seen him, and now so has another. He has to die because he won't stop, Abbie. He's endangering us all by taking down humans like this."

"Then I guess you have no choice," she answered dully, hating it, hating the situation. Why it had to be Harley, she didn't know, but it seemed unfair to saddle him with so much responsibility.

"No," he agreed. "There is no choice.

She looked over to the side for a minute, searching for something to study in the room. It was a nice room, with dark wooden furniture and some pretty antiques on shelves along the beige-colored walls. It was a masculine room, and she could imagine Killian and Harley sitting at the desk, going over whatever business, they had.

"Are you still angry with me?"

The half smile disappeared. "Do you really want to know?"

She nodded. "Of course."

"No."

She pursed her lips and waited for more. When there wasn't any, she raised her eyes to his face. "No? That's all?"

"Don't be pushy," he growled. "You'll get more than you've bargained for."

"Jesus." She slid off his lap and carefully straightened her pants. "Fine. Forget that. But I want you to know I'm complaining. Officially. I don't like this situation with that…that…person." She pointed accusingly at the folder on the desk. "I don't like it at all."

"Don't worry." He pulled her down by the end of her braid for a quick kiss. His other hand absently rubbed against her hip. "Don't worry, I promise everything is going to be all right."

"You can't promise that," she pointed out. "And I can't seem to stop worrying."

"You could try."

She sighed and pulled away from him, already missing his warmth as she headed for the door. "And you could pose nude for me, but that's never going to happen either."

He suddenly straightened in the chair. "What?"

CHAPTER 33

She finished her day by playing video games with Ryan. He was inordinately pleased that she agreed, and soon they were in front of the television, each mashing on the buttons of their controller.

"Fuck," he grumbled. "You're better at this than I expected."

She laid the last finishing move on his avatar and smirked. "Serves you right," she said.

"Goddammit!" He threw the controller at the TV and sat fuming. "This is jacked up!"

She hit the pause button and folded her hands. "Don't get all grumpy because I'm better at this than you."

He attacked her, his hands tickling her stomach and back. She fell over, laughing and giggling, and felt happy for the first time since she woke up. Her fear and nervousness for Harley were forgotten, even for a while.

Harley came to bed that night after one am. She rolled over groggily as he slid into the bed, reaching for him. "What time is it?"

"Shhhh," he whispered, biting her neck gently.

Her desire roared up. She was desperate, wanting the feel of him deep inside her where the yearning burned. The need for him was so strong that she could hardly wait. He kissed her hard, his lips forcing hers to open as his tongue took over, making her groan and cry with want.

"Harley, I need you." She arched as his hand cupped her breast and rubbed over the nipple.

"Shh." He slid up, his cock huge and pulsing against her stomach. He lowered his hand and cupped her heat, pushing a finger inside her to test her readiness. "You're so wet, Abbie."

She cried out, her voice harsh and rough with arousal, telling him how much she wanted him. With his teeth bared, he pulled his finger out of her. "Good enough to eat," he growled. "But that's later. Right now, I'm going to love you, my beauty." He positioned his cock and with a slight thrust, sank halfway into her depths, only to pull out again, and sink in the rest of the way.

She was breathing hard, the heat burning her from the inside out as he pushed inside her, whispering against her ear, telling her how beautiful she was, how tight she was, and how hard he was going to cum. He touched her with his hands and mouth, each caress starting a little fire along her skin until her whole body was ablaze.

"So beautiful," he murmured again, and he swooped down, taking her mouth firmly.

"I'm close," she whispered, shuddering as he increased his speed and depth. He caressed her neck with his fingers and dragged his hand down, tracing the center line of her chest, through the valley of her breasts. He smiled when her breath locked in her lungs and lunged into her harder until he felt the answering spasms of her tight inner muscles.

She came hard, harder than ever before, each shudder wringing a soft moan from her throat. It went on forever, lasting through his orgasm, and then some. Even afterward, she felt a shadow of the climax as she lay in bed, clinging to him because she needed his closeness.

He rolled off, taking her with him as he settled onto his back. Content, she cuddled into his side, her body completely boneless with satisfaction.

"I want to marry you."

She lifted her head from his shoulder and blinked the sleep away. "What?"

He turned toward her. "I want to marry you."

A wave of cold swept her body, causing her to shiver suddenly. "I don't think that would be a good idea." She pushed away from him and sat up against the pillows.

"Why?" he questioned, his voice tight with tension. "Because I'm not a Catholic?"

She pushed her hair behind her back and shook her head absently. "No. I didn't even think about that. I'm more worried about the normal stuff. We haven't been together long enough, Harley and no matter what you said before, you are still angry with me."

"I love you. You know that. What else is there?"

Her heart palpitated slightly as his words sank into her soul. "Well..." She bit her lip in thought and tried to get back on track. "I guess the everyday stuff that most couples face. Generally, people date for years before getting married, and there's a reason. They figure out everything about each other before getting married so they're sure. I'm not going anywhere, there's no reason to rush this."

He sat up on his knees, facing her. "I want you to marry me, Abbie, and not in a few years. I need you to belong to me in every way possible. If you were Were, I wouldn't ask and I wouldn't push for this. We'd already be completely married in the ways of my people, but you're human, and I want that piece of paper that says you're mine."

"Harley, it's not necessary." She inched toward him cautiously, knowing she was causing him further pain by refusing. "I won't leave you again. I promise." She waited, but he said nothing. "Harley?"

"I'll bargain with you," he said, his tone biting. "If I win the challenge against Jaxon, you marry me. If I lose, you don't."

She blinked in the dark for a minute, hoping she'd heard him wrong. *She hadn't.*

"Uh, if you lose, you're dead. This isn't such a good bargain."

He slid closer, his face just an inch away. "Are you saying you don't want me dead?"

She felt like hitting him, but she wasn't that brave yet. "Don't be silly," she said breathlessly, as his lips brushed against her, feathering kisses along her jaw. "You know I don't want you dead. I've never even said anything close to that."

"Excellent," he murmured. "Then we have a bargain. When I win, you will agree to marry me."

"I'm a modern woman. I don't need to be married." She'd always thought about it, wondered but this was beyond anything she'd ever come up with. God. Marriage. And by the tone of his voice and the determination in his eyes, he wouldn't stop until she said yes. And for some reason, that caused her fear and a strong sense of elation.

"I want marriage," he replied darkly. "And because of that, I'll have your promise tomorrow, after the challenge."

"Tomorrow? " she practically shrieked, marriage completely forgotten as the fear of losing him rose strong. "So soon?"

He brought his mouth to hers and kissed her shock away. "Tomorrow," he repeated softly, as he spread her body beneath his. "Now attend to my needs, my love."

He gave her no option other than to please him, and with the approaching dawn, she became desperate for him. *He could die.* Her heart fluttered with the knowledge, and she clung to him as he entered her, knowing it could be her last time with him.

Early in the morning, she opened her eyes to find him looming over her, his face taut and his eyes wild.

She touched his face reverently, lovingly. "You're leaving."

He nodded and leaned down, pressing his lips between her breasts. The feel of his cock jutting was impossible to resist. Knowing where he was about to go, she sat up and pushed him to his back. He rolled over and pulled her on top of him.

"I know you," she murmured sleepily against his neck, rubbing herself against his erection and humming softly with pleasure. He felt so good against her. She'd miss that if he didn't survive. "Sometimes it scares me how well I know you. Better than anyone else, I think."

"We're mated," he crooned, grasping her hips and increasing the pressure as she slid over his cock. "This is how it is for us. This is how it will always be."

She spread her legs even wider and moaned, feeling the tip of his cock teasing her entrance. She shifted just so, and when he next rubbed her up his length, she canted her hips and sighed as he slipped in fully. And then because she had to, she kissed him, licking his mouth as delicately as she could manage. When he growled and sucked at her tongue, she laughed and sat up, loving the feeling of so much heat and strength inside her.

"I'll miss you," she breathed, lifting and lowering her body in a steady rhythm.

"Harder, love." He held her up longer and then thrust his hips up as she was coming down, making them both gasp and causing the tightening deep in her belly to suddenly tighten more.

"Do it again," she breathed, lifting. He thrust, and she went down. The tightness grew dangerously tighter.

She leaned down, flicking her tongue into his mouth as she clung to him and rocked, loving the way he felt deep inside her. More and more and more, until finally she couldn't stand anymore. His cock, so deep, hit just the right place, and suddenly she stiffened and cried out, her muscles pulsating against him, pulling at him. Milking his cock.

He swore and roughly clasped her, jerking her hips up and down until his eyes changed and his mouth twisted with tension. He went over with a sharp cry, with his head thrust back and his body stiffened. Deep inside, she felt the resulting pulsing of his release.

She sank into his chest, breathing hard.

CHAPTER 34

He reached up, his hand moving to the bedside table. She groaned and fell to the side, still holding onto him. "Don't go yet," she said, snuggling up against him. "Just a little longer."

"Shh," he murmured, taking her hand in his. "I have some time."

"Okay," she whispered and fell asleep.

She woke later that morning, and he was gone. She was forced to stay in the bathroom longer than necessary, partly because of the nausea, partly because of the terror she felt over losing him, but also because of the ring she'd discovered on her finger. It was no big diamond or anything flashy, but old, and finely made in silver, with a small yellow stone at the center of a woven-vine band. It was simple and elegant—perfect and it fit.

She stared at it for another minute, marveling at him. And she'd thought he was getting ready to leave when he'd reached over to the nightstand. *Tricky man.* Feeling brave, she left it on while she dressed. He'd given it to her, after all, and it was just a ring, even if it were on the designated ring finger. Besides, she didn't want to hurt him by refusing his gift, so it was only right that she wore it. After her bout with nausea in the bathroom, she shuffled downstairs and encountered Killian in the kitchen. He looked as miserable as she felt but perked up when he saw her.

He slid a cup of tea over as she sat down, then cocked his hip and smiled smugly.

"Excellent. He's finally asked." He stared pointedly at the ring on her finger.

"You can relax," she said tiredly. "I haven't agreed to anything yet."

"But you will. He's not exactly one to accept no as an answer," he said knowingly. "And you're wearing it. That must mean something, don't you think?"

She studied the ring for a moment. "Was it your wife's?"

He shook his head. "No. She favored a more contemporary style. I have hers still, and when Ryan chooses, I hope he'll use it. That particular ring," he nodded at her hand, "belonged to my mother. She was a fine lady; unlike any I've ever met. Harley felt this would suit you best."

"It does," she murmured. "It's perfect." She looked up at his face, studying him.

"You should have told me the challenge was today."

He flinched slightly and refilled his coffee cup. "Yes. But none of us wanted to worry you. I won't lie to you this could end with Harley dead. Jaxon's strong but then, so is Harley, and he's just as ruthless and vicious as any I've known. It'll be a close fight."

Her heart did its fluttering thing again, and she felt weak with it. He could die. How would she survive it?

"What time do we leave?"

He glanced at the clock. "In two hours. The Elders will want to question you and need time to do so. And I always prefer to be there early rather than late."

She tapped her fingers on the countertop, trying to picture the gathering, but her mind wasn't up to it. There was still one more aspect she needed an answer.

"Are they going to be changed?" she asked carefully.

"Some will," he said. "Some won't. Harley will be shifted of course, as will Jaxon. Other than that, it's a personal choice. Ryan will change, he always does. I won't."

"Thank you."

He bowed his head slightly. "It's my pleasure, Abbie."

She dressed heavily for the meeting, putting on as many layers as she could fit under her jacket. Killian came prepared for cold weather, but Ryan only wore a heavy flannel.

At her raised eyebrows, he only shrugged. "Our body temp goes up when we shift."

The drive was tense. Killian seemed especially agitated as he drove to their destination and replied tersely to Ryan's questions. Abbie wisely chose to stay quiet during the drive and watched silently as the sky darkened to the constant night of winter.

Killian pulled into someone's driveway. At least, she *thought* it was a driveway. It was so old and overgrown it was difficult to tell at first. As they drove down, she saw an old house, abandoned by the look of it, and two outbuildings, although they were in disrepair. Everything else was just trees and woods and empty spaces. He pulled in next to the barn and turned off the car. There were already what looked to be forty other vehicles there.

They got out, and she immediately felt the sharp cold. Ryan didn't seem bothered by the icy breeze blowing, but then again neither did Killian. Both men looked directly toward the woods, their focus on the coming battle and the gathering of their pack.

"Come on," Killian ordered, no longer the nice older gentleman of whom she was so fond. He was domineering and autocratic, one powerful enough to hold the position of pack leader for years. She couldn't help but feel a tingle of alarm as she followed them into the woods. He let Ryan lead, staying next to her the entire time, keeping her safe and pointing out obstacles in the path as they walked. Occasionally he'd nod to other pack members, but he was intent on his purpose, which was keeping her healthy and whole.

The forest they entered was ancient, with huge trees, and vines growing around and through the branches, wild and curled everywhere. It was like a completely separate world, she thought. This place of all places was right, untouched, and wild as it was intended. The path grew more and more narrow, and thicker with snow as they went. She had trouble more than once, only to be saved by Killian's strong arms lifting her out of a drift or over a thick branch. No one else seemed to have that problem, even Ryan was focused on moving forward. They finally broke from the path and poured into a clearing, overhung completely with trees that formed a dome that opened in the middle. The sky was visible through the hole in the canopy, dark and heavy with clouds. She stared at it for a minute, wondering how they knew when the moon was full if they couldn't see it.

"Stay by my side, lass," Killian cautioned, as they stood at the back. She nodded, feeling her heart beating too quickly. No one had shifted yet, but she could feel that wild energy that seemed to surround those who were Were, and she took it seriously.

"Ryan," he ordered. "Let Harley know we're in."

He nodded and ran off to the other side of the clearing. She followed his movements and saw him stop before three older men, bow regally, and then move off to the side, where Harley stood alone, large, dark, and imposing.

"God, he's beautiful," she murmured.

Killian's heart melted at her whispered tone. "Have you told him you love him?"

She looked over at him, and almost panicked look on her face. "What?"

"You love him," he said simply. "He's always been lacking in love. His mother abandoned him when he was young, and I think that left a scar. He needs love, Abbie, perhaps more than anyone I've ever known."

She turned away from him and wrapped her arms tighter around her waist. "I don't know him well enough."

Yet her words from early that morning echoed in her ears as if to refute what she'd said.

He tilted his head and watched her, noting her worried expression and the pain in her eyes. "I knew my wife for one day before I fell in love with her, she was my heart. When she died, I knew there was no use in trying to replace her. I love her still, and I will until I die. It's not always like that, mind you, but with Harley, I have no doubt he will love just as fully as I did."

Just then, a young woman came through the crowd. She was tall, nearly six feet, with long blonde hair and deep blue eyes. She bowed regally to Killian, then looked at Abbie. "They will see you now."

Abbie reached for Killian. He grasped her hand tightly and followed her through the crowd as she followed the other woman. She kept her head down, didn't look at the others as she made her way, and tried to figure out what she would say.

The woman stopped them before the three old gentlemen. Each looked like he was over eighty-five, and each had hard eyes, full of memories of the glory of youth.

"This is the woman?" the one on the left asked, turning his head to Harley.

"It is," he answered, staring coolly at Abbie.

"She's rather small, isn't she?"

She frowned at the old man. "You're not large, either." And he wasn't. They were all three shrunk with age. It was rude to her for them to point fingers.

"True," he sighed. "But I haven't always been like this."

She let that go and waited. It didn't take long.

"We wish to know about this Were you saw," the one in the middle said, his voice breathy with age. "Tell us of that night."

Behind her, Killian squeezed her hand reassuringly. She started haltingly. It was difficult to recount such a personal tale to utter strangers. At some point, she found herself watching Harley, and from that point on, she grew more comfortable and finished the story without crying.

"And you're sure Jaxon was this Were, this animal you saw that night?" a man asked from the side. He had a hostile look in his eyes like he blamed her for the proceedings.

She frowned but directed her answer to the Elders. "I thought about this also," she said. "I drew several pictures of him after it happened, so his image has remained fresh. But also, I'm sure because of what Elijah Haren said several days ago, during a botched attempt to kidnap me."

"We've heard the tale," the middle one said. "So, you didn't pinpoint Jaxon as your attacker of that night."

"No," she said. "But I believe it is him. I recognized him in the pictures Harley showed me."

The old men all nodded in tandem. One of them said, "You are dismissed." The man at the side took her place before them and started arguing fiercely. She didn't wait to hear what he was saying and happily let Killian lead her away. The people looked ordinary, even boring; she decided as she looked over the gathered crowd as they passed through. Some were tall, others weren't. Some were heavy, and others weren't. Some were men, some were women. She would have never picked any of them out as werewolves, but their combined energy was familiar and reminded her of the night in the pub. That had been what was off with them. It wasn't anything visible, just a sense, and it grew stronger when they gathered together.

CHAPTER 35

Abbie and Killian were on one side of the clearing when suddenly there was a huge indrawn breath from the crowd. She stood on her tiptoes, trying to see over everyone, and caught sight of a tall nude form striding around the circle left bare in the middle of the clearing. He was tall and lanky, with muscled arms and chest, and red hair and beard. He was attractive, if a little boring with it. He bowed low to them all. "My people," he said in a rich baritone voice, a smile on his lips. Then he looked through the crowd at Abbie and blew her a kiss. She stumbled back and turned to Killian. "Did he do what I think he did?"

His eyes were hard as he turned to her. "He did," he growled low. There was another collective breath, and then she saw a shadow move forward, large, and dark. Harley seemed to glide; his steps were so smooth. He too was nude as he stepped within the circle, and the differences between the two men were obvious. Harley, too, was muscular and tall, but he was thicker and built heavier. He was built for endurance, whereas Jaxon was more high-spirited. Harley didn't bow, but looked around the crowd, like a king viewing his subjects.

The three old men stepped forward, almost a single entity. The one in the middle seemed to be the speaker for the other two as they faced the pack and meted out their decision.

"We hereby declare this challenge binding and subject to those laws that govern the pack. Jaxon Haren is hereby censured by the Elders and turned over to the formal challenge of pack leader."

And that was it. The minute they were done speaking, the battle began.

A long howl suddenly cut through the clearing. Abbie jerked her head over and saw Harley, in the center of the circle with his head thrown back, his arms held out at his sides. His flesh rippled, and like some horrible experiment gone wrong, he began to change before her eyes, his muscles and bones shifting with painful cracks and groans, his nose and mouth elongating, making room for rows of sharp teeth, and his legs bending and breaking, only to reshape themselves as he fell to the ground on all fours. All along his body, thick, black hair sprouted. In Were form, he was just as huge as she'd remembered and just as frightening. Others in the crowd began to change, although it wasn't everyone. Those who did fell to all fours and completed their transitions as if it were nothing unusual. And it wasn't, she supposed. Not one person looked at them oddly. More and more howls joined the first until the forest was filled with their sounds of joy and sorrow as first Harley, and then others rose, completely shifting over.

She stepped back as the creatures got up, suddenly taller and larger than she could scarcely believe. Different colors of pelts were mixed in with the other human forms swathed in heavy jackets, from the blackest of blacks to the palest creams. Size differed from creature to creature, but everyone dwarfed her and was armed with lethal claws and fangs that were sharp enough to kill in a single bite.

"Relax," Killian said beside her, his face unchanged and as kind as she remembered. "None of them will hurt you. It's simply a shift in the skin. Their hearts and personalities remain the same, even if they do become a bit more wild."

She nodded. "Right," she breathed, trying to convince herself. Then the fight started, and she forgot everything else. "Come on. We need to go forward. I want to see everything."

They went through the crowd, moving slowly through the sea of bodies. Abbie kept her eyes on the ring in the center, wincing and looking away every few seconds, but unable to witness the fight. Jaxon attacked Harley first, coming so quick and strong that he was thrown to his back forced to fight Jaxon off with claws and teeth. She was crying within minutes.

He screamed in pain as the copper Were scraped his claws down his side, and then he roared and threw him off. He flipped to his feet, and prowled around the circle, ignoring the crowd chanting surrounding him.

"We've got to get closer," Abbie gasped, even as Killian tried pulling her back. She shook her head at him and pushed forward, searching for a better vantage. When she saw a spot just outside the ring, she took it, pulling Killian close behind her. Jaxon attacked again, aiming low, but this time Harley was ready and swiped at him with his claws. Jaxon grunted but gave no indication he was hit as he jumped back and prepared for another attack, circling slowly. He fell to all fours and stood completely still; his lip lifted in a snarl. Harley lowered himself, and just as his front legs touched the ground, Jaxon attacked, charging forward, and plowing into Harley, taking him to his back. They snarled fiercely, clawing and ripping at each other. Jaxon stayed on top, holding Harley down, his muzzle inches from his throat. When he finally lunged forward, Harley turned just slightly, but enough. Jaxon latched onto his shoulder, his teeth going deep even as bone snapped, and tissue tore through.

"Harley!" Abbie yelled, her heart-stopping as the terrible noises reached her ears. It was like nothing she'd ever heard, awful crunching and gurgling as blood collected in Jaxon's throat. She would hear that sound in her nightmares. Jaxon growled deep and clenched his jaw even tighter. Harley's head fell back as he screamed with pain, even as his hand came up and smashed against Jaxon's side, jarring both of them with the impact. There was another snap as Jaxon rolled away, the jerk of his teeth breaking another bone in Harley's shoulder.

Jaxon was already up, waiting for Harley to roll to his feet. When he did, he wavered slightly. His eyes went over the crowd quickly, and when they landed on her, they stayed for a minute. Abbie's knees nearly gave out. He turned back to the center of the ring, his one shoulder useless, his side ripped open from Jaxon's claws. He stood there, looking beaten down like she'd never seen him look before. *Broken.*

"You can yield," Jaxon muttered thickly, stalking forward. "But I'd still kill you."

"Then fight and finish it."

They charged, and somehow Harley managed to throw him off, so far he bowled into the crowd, knocking over pack members, causing some of them to yip in fright and pain. With a savage curse, he got to his feet, scraping his claws over the chest of one who didn't move, snarling at the rest in warning. Then he turned back to the circle, his eyes glinting evilly in the pale light. His head fell back in a howl, and then he ran forward, diving toward Harley, who moved back at the last second and swiped his claws down Jaxon's back.

"Killian," Abbie said worriedly, her eyes locked on the scene. "This is not going well." She squeezed his hand as the Weres went for each other, again meeting in the center. Again, Jaxon went down, but it was close this time, with Harley nearly losing his balance and falling onto his damaged shoulder. "Killian—"

"I know," he said hoarsely.

In the circle, Jaxon got up slowly, his back open nearly to the bone. His breathing was hard, and his head hung low for a second. Then he moved sideways around Harley, who stood still in the center. When Jaxon moved again, it was too fast for her to see. He dodged low, his claws going for the soft tissue of Harley's stomach, he snarled and didn't allow it.

He lunged forward, snapping at his opponent's throat. But it was his clawed hand that did the most damage, wrapping around and digging through the already flayed layers of skin and muscle of Jaxon's back until he connected with his spine. He shoved his claws through it, shattering nerves, and vertebrae, and with a vicious tug, he severed it completely, dragging out a length of the shiny bone and leaving it to sparkle dully in the night.

Jaxon's body stiffened in shock and pain, his eyes going wide for a minute just as a scream of defeat poured from his throat.

Harley leaped away from his opponent, scraped and bleeding, but the victor. Jaxon crumpled to the ground and lay still, gasping for breath, his eyes rolling to the back of his head. After a minute, his body gave up the fight, and he died.

Abbie didn't know at what point she fell, but suddenly was hoisted up by Killian and carried forward. He said nothing to the other pack members as he entered the circle with her securely in his arms.

Harley's head swung around and growled, his lips lifting in warning. Killian stopped just inside the circle; every muscle tight with tension. "I'm bringing her to you, Alpha. I'm bringing you your mate."

When he took another step Harley's growl deepened but his eyes were on Abbie.

"Put me down," she whispered, loosening her hold on Killian's neck as he let her feet touch the ground. Carefully, she walked forward, tears running down her cheeks as she reached for him. The minute her fingers touched his body, she collapsed against him. His uninjured arm curled around her back, holding her to him tightly. Every fear she'd ever had about being terrified of him while he was changed completely slipped from her head. She clung to him, wrapping her hands in his thick pelt as she felt for herself that he was healthy if a bit beat up. His arm and shoulder were a complete ruin, as was his side, but he seemed otherwise to be well. From the crowd, one of the Weres howled. Harley's head fell back and joined in, and she couldn't do anything except wrap her arms around his thick neck and hold onto him for all she was worth.

The call went on and on and then suddenly the crowd surged forward, bowing to him, and wishing him prosperity and many cubs. She hid her head farther in his neck and waited for it to be over wanting nothing except to go home and sleep.

"You're hurt," she whispered against his chest, once the shifted Weres had run off the unchanged were intent on shifting and joining a hunt.

"I'll live," he growled out, his changed mouth working oddly to create the words. She wiggled enough that he released her, but she stayed near his side, watching him in case his loss of blood and injury suddenly took its toll. "Where's Killian?" she asked, searching the crowd for his familiar form. "We need to get you home. You're going to need stitches, I think."

But he didn't hear her. His eyes were staring through the woods, his body tensing as the sounds of the Weres crashing through the underbrush and chasing God-only-knew reached his ears.

"Harley?" She brushed her hand against his chest, and nearly screeched when his head abruptly turned toward her. "What's wrong?"

"I have to go."

"But—your injuries." She stared pointedly at his shoulder, at the blood that was running freely down. "Harley, you're hurt."

A high-pitched yip filled the air, and he quickly dropped to all fours, his head pointing in the direction it'd come.

She held onto his fur, grasping it thickly at his back. "Harley, don't. Please, don't leave me like this."

He turned to her briefly but was ready to go, his body thrumming with energy.

"I'll come for you tonight. Ryan!"

Her fingers loosened on him just seconds before he ran from her, his large body rippling with muscle as he ran through the woods, faster than anything she'd ever seen. Just before disappearing, he met up with a similarly large, brown Were. Together, they chased into the trees, and then they were gone.

"They can't help it," Killian said, coming up behind her with a funny smile.

"I raised both of my boys to embrace their dual natures. I believe I succeeded, but perhaps a bit too well."

She shook her head, her worry still too fresh. "His shoulder. Killian, he's hurt. *He almost lost.* He probably has broken ribs to go along with the shoulder, and his side was ripped up, too."

"He'll heal and I doubt that he was quite as weakened as he appeared. He's a smart man. He'd make an advantage out of an injury if it suited his purposes."

"Are you sure?" She looked at him pleadingly before returning to the trees they'd disappeared in. "Can he get help if he suddenly goes down?"

He smiled. "The entire pack is with him, Abbie. He's safe. Now, you and I are heading home where an excellent apple pie waiting for us and a strong cup of tea. After this week, I need it."

She took the arm he offered and reluctantly walked away from the clearing, the excited sounds of the Weres hunting ringing in her ears.

CHAPTER 36

Near midnight, she was wide awake, her eyes pasted to the window leading out to the front. So far, there was nothing, but she felt sure he'd show.

"I was wondering about the type of wedding you'd care for me to plan. I was thinking of something simple and elegant, with just a few friends and family." Killian frowned and looked up from the notepad he was scribbling in. "I do hope your mother won't be able to make it, however. I fear meeting her. What do you think?"

She turned her head. "Hmm? What was that?"

"The wedding. Your mother. Fear of meeting her. What are your thoughts on all this?"

"Oh God. Please tell me you're not going to start in on all this." She turned back to the window; sure, she'd seen something move. But there was nothing, just a partial moon and an empty yard. "You're supposed to be on my side for this. There's no reason we have to rush getting married."

"Oh, you'll marry him and sooner than you realize. Now, as I was saying, it won't be more than a hundred people. We'll have to speak to someone immediately about a dress for you, and of course a florist—"

"Killian," she said, swinging around and pinning him with her coldest stare, "The most he's going to manage to do is get me before a justice of the peace. I'd dye my hair orange before I do a wedding, as I'm sure you already know."

He smiled in satisfaction and leaned back in his chair. "Just so you realize you will be getting married. It's a shame really, though. I do enjoy a wedding, and I know so few humans. I wish the Weres had adopted the practice."

She let his voice drone on and turned to the window, anxious to see something. Anything. Harley had promised. She just hoped he didn't wait until four in the morning to fulfill it.

Her eyes wandered over the yard, and after a time she turned back to the living room, her eyes getting heavy as she stared at the crackling fire. Killian smiled at her and turned back to his notebook, a fresh glass of cognac at his elbow. Minutes before the clock struck two, Killian's head lifted, and his eyes got that faraway look he adopted when his wild side rose.

"They're back."

She got slowly to her feet and looked out the window. There, just in the distance, a shaggy form stood, pale brown in the moonlight, and just beyond him, there was another darker, larger, and more fierce.

"I'll get your coat," he said.

The air was beyond brisk, beyond cold. It was fucking freezing. Abbie stopped just beyond the porch and stared into the woods even as Harley's dark body slinked forward. He was still on all fours, his back bent as his body hunched down.

"Harley?"

He trotted forward, coming at her quickly. She started to scream even as he halted in front of her and buried his head in her stomach. Her knees gave out and she sank to the ground, the frozen snow and wind completely forgotten.

"Are you okay?"

He hunkered down with her. Even lying on his stomach as he was doing his head was almost level with hers. She felt ridiculously small like a child playing with an Alaskan Huskey.

"We hunted."

She leaned down and laid her head against his neck, her hands digging into his soft fur. "What now? What do we do?"

"You will marry me."

She held her breath, and then let it out slowly with a sigh. "Yes. I will marry you."

"I want the words, Abbie."

She lifted her head and looked into his odd eyes. She knew what he was asking for because she wanted to say them as much as he wanted to hear them. "I love you," she whispered.

A rumble came from his chest as he laid his head in her lap, his clawed hands clenching gently against her legs as he inhaled her scent. "I want to love you, like this in my pelt."

"Now?" She looked around but saw no one. It was still unnerving, though. The house was right there, and she knew Ryan was somewhere close. "Harley, they'll see."

"Now." He got up on all fours, his fingers slipping into the waist of her sweatpants and pushing them down. "I need you," he growled.

She shook, but she allowed him to remove her pants and underwear. He left the rest of her clothes alone, although she suspected that was more for protection against the cold than any desire on his part.

He positioned her knees on her discarded sweats, and pushed her to her hands, already rising behind her. His cock brushed against her bare legs. She shivered, but not from the cold.

"It's going to be fast," he snarled, pushing her legs wider. "And hard."

She nodded, watching him over her shoulder. She should have been terrified. Here she was, about to screw around with a creature that rightfully belonged in her nightmares, yet she couldn't seem to get past the lust. It was there, as always, just beneath the surface, waiting only for the slightest hint from Harley. She wiggled her hips at him. "I'm waiting," she breathed. He laughed throatily, the sound coming out more like a threat than something signaling amusement. Slowly, he pushed his cock forward. He didn't stop until he was inside her to the hilt.

He stayed still, his hands locked on her hips, the fur of his pelt rubbing against her thighs and lower back. "We're to have a baby."

She closed her eyes, the cold of the snow barely even a thought compared to his heat deep inside her. "I know."

And suddenly, he started fucking her, and just as he'd promised, it was rough, fast, and hard. She loved every glorious minute of it.

BONUS MATERIAL

A missing best friend. A dangerous underworld. A temptation she can't resist.

When Serenity Kline receives a desperate call from her missing best friend, she'll do whatever it takes to bring her back even if it means stepping into a shadowy world ruled by vampires. Determined to save her from becoming a feeder, Serenity leaves her quiet life behind and dives into a seductive underworld where humans surrender their will to powerful vampire masters.

Damien Shaw is more than just a vampire guardian he's sworn to protect humans. The moment he meets Serenity; he knows she doesn't belong in his world. Yet her fiery determination and intoxicating allure make him crave her in ways he can't ignore.

As Serenity poses as Damien's submissive feeder to infiltrate the vampire elite, she discovers a shocking truth: surrendering control to him awakens a freedom she never knew she craved. And for Damien, just one taste of her blood leaves him yearning for more… more of her, and only her.

But their bond is as dangerous as it is undeniable. The deeper Damien pulls Serenity into his world, the harder it becomes to protect her from the darkness that threatens to consume them both.

Will their forbidden desire save her friend or destroy them both?

ABOUT THE AUTHOR

Jezza Deep is a versatile indie author whose captivating stories span genres and audiences. Jezza's tales are rich with emotion, mysticism, and unforgettable characters, from the steamy Fractured Desires Trilogy to the enchanting YA series Fires Within.

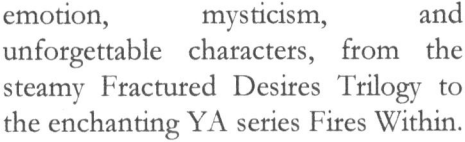

Her literary debut, Seven of Sins, boldly explores the seven deadly sins and offers a powerful story of redemption through love. She continued to thrill readers with Recapturing Fate and charmed younger audiences with her magical Bedtime Stories for Children series.

Jezza's poetry, recognized internationally with works featured in the International Library of Poetry, showcases the same creativity and depth found in her fiction. She's also a passionate advocate for the anime community, blending her love for storytelling with insightful critique.

Whether through fractured fairy tales, fan fiction, or novels, Jezza's unique voice transcends boundaries, leaving a lasting impression on readers of all ages. Follow her journey as she continues to create stories that inspire, enchant, and delight.